THE WOMAN
in the
WARDROBE

Mr Verity

THE WOMAN
in the
WARDROBE

*P*ETER *S*HAFFER

With a preface by
ELINOR SHAFFER

and an introduction by
MARTIN EDWARDS

Nicolas Bentley drew the pictures

This edition published 2020 by
The British Library
96 Euston Road
London
NW1 2DB

The Woman in the Wardrobe was first published under the penname
'Peter Antony' in 1951 by Evans Brothers Ltd, London.

Cataloguing in Publication Data

A catalogue record for this book is available from the British Library

ISBN 978 0 7123 5346 5
eISBN 978 0 7123 6776 9

Typeset by Tetragon, London
Printed in England by TJ International, Padstow, Cornwall

CONTENTS

PREFACE

Anthony and Peter Shaffer, twin sons (b. 1926) of Jacob and Reka Shaffer, were called, like other boys of their wartime generation, to support the war effort by going down the coal mines as "Bevin Boys". Tony, who always assumed and was accorded the role of elder brother, managed the arduous underground work in the mines, but Peter fell ill, and bore the traces for the rest of his life. Nevertheless, they completed their war service and went up to Trinity College, Cambridge, in 1947, together with their brother Brian, three years younger and coming straight from St. Paul's School. Tony read law, Peter, history; their younger brother read natural sciences. They wrote some pieces for College magazines, and Peter submitted a story to the well-known writer E.M. Forster, a Fellow of King's College; it was not accepted for publication, as it was deemed too long, but Forster wrote a very appreciative and constructive set of comments on the young man's story, and invited him to tea. Peter was amazed and delighted, as an unpublished note of the period shows, that the famous novelist was so civil to him and spoke to him as to a fellow writer.[1]

The two brothers were fans of detective stories in that heyday of detective fiction, stemming from G.K. Chesterton if not from Sherlock Holmes, and during their student days coinciding with the popularity of Agatha Christie and the long-standing Detection Club, founded in 1930 after notable examples of the genre had appeared, they enjoyed imagining stories in the style of the genre. The inter-war years had been called "the golden age of detective fiction" by John Strachey in 1939;[2] but the "age of detective fiction" was far from over.

Essential was to invent a detective who could vie with Christie's Hercule Poirot, the dapper Belgian detective who always bested the dull-witted police and unmasked the malefactor dramatically from a large cast of suspects. Who could do this more dramatically than their invented detective, the learned, wilful and eloquent Mr Verity? A domestic setting was often the place of the murder, with a large cast of suspects, some of whom were concealing their pasts. A particular room in the house was the scene of the murder; whether drawing room, bedroom, dining room, or library, and who had access to it, when and how, was often key to the solution. The murder weapon was also a vital component. So, in *The Woman in the Wardrobe* the body is not simply in a room, it is in a wardrobe in a room; why? How many keys are needed? Who had access to them? to the room? to the wardrobe? The solution is magnificently complex and triumphantly convincing, delivered with the required brio by the sleuth. The two brothers called their invented author by the twinning pseudonym, Peter Antony.

Tony was a fount of elaborate, hilarious and over-the-top plot ideas, and he and Peter shared in the fun; but when it came to writing, it was Peter who carried it out, smoothly, proportionately, and believably. Tony's memoir *So What Did You Expect?* confirms that Peter was the author, the sole writer of the book; and it was with Peter alone that the contract with the then publisher was drawn up.

In later years, Peter saw and defined himself simply and proudly as a playwright, and his career as a playwright he dated from the London production of *Five Finger Exercise* in 1958, which won the Evening Standard Drama Award. Works, even plays, written before that date he grouped together casually and dismissively—"there had been some for television and radio before that", he wrote in the preface to his *Collected Plays* in 1982, referring in this phrase to the detective novels, to a TV drama (his excellent *The Salt Land*, shown on ABC TV in New York in 1955), and radio plays perhaps still to be rediscovered.[3]

Nevertheless, a thread of the early fascination with mysterious or inexplicable actions, threatening events even including murder, and alternative modes of unravelling a strange event still run through his most serious and challenging dramatic works.

Five Finger Exercise, a well-made family drama, itself ends with a death, a suicide, but one brought about through a complex plot by others (indeed revealing both an individual plot and a world-historical issue); *Equus*, revolving around the blinding of six horses by a young man (based on an actual court case related to Peter by a magistrate) and a complex unravelling of the circumstances and the forces as understood by a psychiatrist in the terms of his own life as well as those of his profession; in *Amadeus*, an interpretation of the life and death of Mozart in terms of a murderous jealousy on the part of a rival musician, Antonio Salieri, who over a period of time intervened disastrously in his career; and one might point to other examples in Peter's oeuvre, including the playscript he left at his death in 2016, centring on the mysterious and much-debated death of Tchaikovsky: was it death by accidental infection during a typhus epidemic, or death by suicide brought about by the provocation and judgement of a self-appointed "court"?

One could add still other examples from his work: was the death of the Inca king at the hands of the conquistador Pizarro in *The Royal Hunt of the Sun* not the murder of one civilisation by another? Later Peter remembered that he had read of the conquest of the Incas while he had been lying in his sickbed after his stint as a Bevin Boy. At the last, is there not a "mortal mystery" behind or within these stories which some call tragedy.

The youthful detective jape thus unfolded itself into world-historical questions. But that does not take away from the sheer hilarity and good spirits that went into the two undergraduates' invention. If Peter quickly came to dismiss his early efforts, and defined himself as a writer for the stage (though many of his plays also came to the screen despite his strong preference for the live theatre), Tony continued in this vein, writing the scripts for Hollywood's versions of two of Agatha Christie's most popular detective fictions, *Murder on the Orient Express* and *Death on the Nile*. We may also recall that much later Peter jumped to the defence of his brother's work when after Tony's death the well-known playwright Harold Pinter requested permission to use Tony's very successful play and film *Sleuth* while rewriting the dialogue himself. Peter refused this permission with considerable anger and indignation and a strong defence of Tony's power and originality, in language as well as plot, as the author of the script.[4] Tony's film *The Wicker Man*, now something of a cult film, still follows the detective thread (indeed, the main character is a police detective); but the hunt is for the victim.

The Woman in the Wardrobe may then still be glimpsed behind the grander edifices that Peter Shaffer constructed over the rest of his life as one of the leading playwrights of the half century following the Second World War.

ELINOR SHAFFER, 2020

ELINOR SHAFFER is Peter Shaffer's sister-in-law, who just before her wedding flew from her teaching post at Berkeley for the opening night of *The Royal Hunt of the Sun* at Chichester, and was present at nearly all the productions of his plays in London as well as the opening on Broadway of *Equus*. She is herself an author and founder of the British Comparative Literature Association.

NOTES

1 Letter from E.M. Forster to Peter Shaffer, 7 March 1948, in the Wren Library Collection of Peter Shaffer's papers, Trinity College, Cambridge.

2 See Martin Edwards, *The Golden Age of Murder* (London: HarperCollins, 2015), p. 9.

3 Preface, *The Collected Plays of Peter Shaffer* (New York: Harmony Books, 1982), p. vii.

4 Peter Shaffer, unpublished letter to Harold Pinter, 18 April 2007, in the Wren Library Collection of Peter Shaffer's papers, Trinity College, Cambridge.

FURTHER READING

Michael Billington, 'Shaffer, Sir Peter Levin (1926–2016)', *Oxford Dictionary of National Biography* (Oxford: Oxford University Press, 2004)

Michael Billington, *State of the Nation: British Theatre since 1945* (London: Faber & Faber, 2007)

Martin Edwards, *The Golden Age of Murder* (London: HarperCollins, 2015)

Peter Shaffer, *The Collected Plays of Peter Shaffer* (New York: Harmony Books, 1982)

Peter Shaffer, *Amadeus. A Play by Peter Shaffer* (London: HarperCollins, 2001)

Peter Shaffer, *Equus* (London: Penguin, 2007) (see also the 1977 film adaptation written by Peter Shaffer and directed by Sidney Lumet)

Peter Shaffer, *My Life in the Theatre: A Memoir*, eds Richard Mayne and Elinor Shaffer (London and New York: Bloomsbury, forthcoming)

INTRODUCTION

The Woman in the Wardrobe is a highly enjoyable whodunit in the classic tradition of the detective story. The novel's young author would eventually become one of Britain's most distinguished playwrights and a knight of the realm. He disguised himself as Peter Antony, but his real name was Peter Shaffer, and today he is more commonly associated with such theatrical successes as *Equus* and *Amadeus*. In his twenties, he produced three detective novels, two of them written in collaboration with his twin brother Anthony. These books are now very rare, and are much sought after by collectors, having been out of print for more than half a century. Thanks to the British Library's policy of rescuing obscure classics of crime fiction, a new generation of readers finally has the chance to relish the delights of this *jeu d'esprit*, a book that served as a form of authorial apprenticeship.

Although the Golden Age of detective fiction is generally regarded as the period between the two world wars, echoes of the Golden Age style and the use of popular Golden Age tropes are to be found in a wide range of books published during the past three-quarters of a century. In their youth, the Shaffer twins devoured Golden Age mysteries, and their own novels followed the traditional pattern, just as did those of later detective novelists such as Patricia Moyes, V.C. Clinton-Baddeley, and Sarah Caudwell, all of whose careers began long after the Golden Age had ended.

The Woman in the Wardrobe looks back, very consciously, to fiction of the past, whereas novels such as Patricia Highsmith's *Strangers on a Train* and Julian Symons' *The Thirty-First of February*, early examples of post-war psychological suspense, appeared the year before Shaffer's debut. In writing his novel, Shaffer's aims were very different from those of Highsmith and Symons. He simply wanted to amuse and entertain, and accordingly sub-titled his debut *A Light-Hearted Detective Story*.

Shaffer's protagonist is a jokey version of the Great Detective beloved of Golden Age authors and their fans. Mr Verity, much-travelled but now a resident of Amnestie in Sussex, "was very much disliked. It was partly because he was so often right. And partly... because he had an inexcusable manner of making himself indispensable in a case, and finally of solving it between tea and supper, with a mixed display of condescension and incivility." He becomes embroiled in a mystery concerning a shooting in a locked room. The late Bob Adey, the foremost expert on this sub-genre of detective fiction, went so far in his definitive guide *Locked Room Murders* as to describe Shaffer's story as "the best postwar locked-room mystery... [with] a brilliant new solution."

Anthony Joshua Shaffer was born in Liverpool on 15 May 1926 at 9.30 a.m. To everyone's surprise, given that the maternity doctor's stethoscope had failed to detect two heartbeats, Peter Levin Shaffer was born five minutes later. The twins had a brother, Brian, three years their junior. The family was affluent, Jewish, and academically gifted. Peter was educated at St Paul's School and Trinity College, Cambridge. In 1951, Evans published *The Woman in the Wardrobe*; although it was a solo effort by Peter, he adopted a pseudonym that combined his name with a version of his twin's. The book benefited from sketches of the main characters by Nicolas Bentley, himself an occasional crime writer as well as an artist; Nicolas was also the son of E.C. Bentley, author of the seminal detective novel *Trent's Last Case* and second President of the Detection Club.

The Woman in the Wardrobe was followed a year later by *How Doth the Little Crocodile*, again authored by Peter Antony, and again featuring Mr Verity, but published by Gollancz. This time, however, the book was a collaboration between the twins. In Anthony's entertaining if highly unreliable memoir *So What Did You Expect?* (2001), he described theirs as "an odd sort of partnership, with me providing the basic plots and Peter and I penning alternate chapters." (One is tempted to speculate that he might have made a minor, unacknowledged contribution to *The Woman in the Wardrobe*, but the publishing contract suggests otherwise; the agreement is with Peter alone.) The third book, published as by A. and P. Shaffer, was *Withered Murder* (1955). Anthony, by then the editor of *The London Mystery Magazine*, cheekily reviewed the book himself in highly enthusiastic terms. Anthony observed in his memoir: "despite this chicanery, sales were comparatively modest, and the books today remain something of a curiosity, though we have *so far* resisted *numerous* offers to republish them."

After that, the twins' literary paths diverged. Peter found his true calling as a man of the theatre. His first major stage success was *Five Finger Exercise*, and later works such as *The Royal Hunt of the Sun*, *Black Comedy*, *Equus*, *Amadeus*, and *Lettice and Lovage* secured his reputation. He was appointed a CBE in 1987 and knighted fourteen years later. Anthony credits Peter with encouraging him to give up a successful and lucrative career in advertising in order to concentrate on writing. A more avowedly commercial writer than his twin, he is best known for the enormously successful detective play *Sleuth*, which illustrates his knowledge and understanding of the genre, in the dialogue as well as in the ingenuity of the plot. He also wrote the influential and critically acclaimed horror film *The Wicker Man* as well as screenplays for big budget films based on novels by Agatha Christie and a script based on a novel by Arthur La Bern, *Goodbye Piccadilly, Farewell Leicester Square*, which became the Hitchcock thriller *Frenzy*.

Anthony died in 2001 and Peter in 2016, at the age of ninety. At the time of Peter's knighthood, the actor Simon Callow described him as "the playwright who forced the mainstream audience to think about the big ideas of their times". There is a distinct shortage of big ideas of the kind Callow had in mind in *The Woman in the Wardrobe* but the story is none the worse for that. Welcome to a detective novel that is straightforward, unashamed fun.

MARTIN EDWARDS

www.martinedwardsbooks.com

THE WOMAN
in the
WARDROBE

To my parents
with deepest love and appreciation

CHAPTER I

T HE LITTLE TOWN OF AMNESTIE HAD NOT KNOWN A death so bloody since the fifteenth century.

The place was in Sussex, and generally classed as a seaside resort: it had borne its name since the Wars of the Roses, when there appear to have been two not very pitched battles on the beach. In the first the Lancastrians drove the Yorkists from the sand-dunes back to the town; in the second the Yorkists drove the Lancastrians from the sand-dunes into the sea. After each engagement there was a general amnesty for a population which, out of a natural desire to maintain its property, had adopted a rather confused neutrality and aided both sides indiscriminately.

From those times the number of inhabitants had risen from fifty to five thousand—quite a considerable advance in five centuries. The nearest proper town was Carrington, four miles away to the East, and boasting twelve thousand.

The main concern of the men of Amnestie was with fish; their main entertainment, the couples who came down from London at week-ends, put up at 'The Charter', and drove off first thing on Monday morning looking uncomfortable. 'The Charter' of Amnestie was quite often in the Sunday papers.

It was a high, white building standing rather apart at the end of the main street. It was easily the most dominating place in the town, and certainly the most comfortable—with the exception of Mr Verity's villa.

As we have a deal to do with Mr Verity—in fact we start with what Mr Verity saw as he watched the front entrance of 'The Charter'—some form of introduction must be attempted.

He was an immense man, just tall enough to carry his breadth majestically. His face was sharp, smooth and teak-brown; his blue eyes small and of a startling brilliance. He wore a fine chestnut Van-Dyck, an habitual cloak in winter and the (some would say cultivated) expression of an elderly 'Laughing Cavalier'. By this time, of course, he had long been a noted figure in the world of detection, and wonderfully respected by the Yard. In fact, if that were possible, almost as much respected as disliked.

For Mr Verity was very much disliked. It was partly because he was so often right. And partly, also, because he had an inexcusable manner of making himself indispensable in a case, and finally of solving it between tea and supper, with a mixed display of condescension and incivility, when the regular police in charge were about dead with fatigue. The thing which no one could excuse this brilliant, lumbering, bearded giant was his amateur enlightenment—the fact that his words spoke so much louder than everybody else's actions.

He lived in his 'villa' just outside Amnestie, on a windy hill overlooking the town: to be truthful, it was little more than three tiny fishing cottages knocked into one low, medium-sized house, but it charmed him. The whole had been whitewashed and named 'Persepolis'. Its living-room, but for the smallest of kitchens, ran the length of the place, and resembled nothing so much as a sculptor's workroom. From the floor sprang a forest of pedestals, each bearing the head or torso (and very occasionally both) of some Ancient notable. Mr Verity had travelled far in his sixty-six years of life, mostly in Classical lands: and where Mr Verity travelled, he rummaged. In fact, he admitted to having more archaeological thefts to his credit than the governing body of any museum in Europe. Marbles were a speciality of his; burial urns a side-line.

One July morning just before eight o'clock, Mr Verity was striding down from 'Persepolis' for an early bathe. A wonder-ful day was beginning to flare in the East: the fretted towers of Carrington were just visible through the haze that clung to the sea, and above him the weather-vane on the church steeple dazzled his eyes as he entered the town. He was just level with 'The Charter' Hotel when he saw something which made him halt in his tracks and retire under the tattered awning of a shop opposite to watch. A man in shirt sleeves was climbing furtively out of a first-floor window. When he had satisfied himself that there was no one about, he walked swiftly along the balcony to the next window, pushed it up, and entered the room which neighboured his own. The window was pulled softly down behind him.

Mr Verity was an abnormally curious man. He was also more than usually experienced: and there was something about this performance that warned him to take notice.

Emerging swiftly from his retirement under the awning, he crossed the road and entered the hotel. A large woman with a heavy face that had been dusted almost casually with powder sat at the hall desk. She was looking through what seemed to be accounts.

"Good morning," said Verity. "Are you the Manageress?"

"Yes?"

"I am pleased to meet you. My name is Verity. I am a resident here. I'm sorry to say I have not made your acquaintance before. In mitigation, however, I must say that I have been busy knocking down my cottages."

"Oh…"

"Yes. Tell me, Miss—"

"Framer."

"Tell me, Miss Framer, whether it is usual for guests at this hotel to use the window as an exit?"

"I'm afraid I don't understand."

Verity repeated his question. Miss Framer suddenly smiled nervously.

"Why no… Of course not…"

"And what would you do if I were to tell you that that is just what someone is doing up on your first floor?"

"What?… But that can't be!… I mean it's highly irregular."

"I'm glad you feel that way about it," said Verity warmly. "And even more irregular if they entered the room next door?"

"Next door?"

Miss Framer rose at once.

"Yes. I watched a man climb out and then in. Quite expertly, too. I'm afraid I don't like it at all."

Miss Framer

"Oh no!" There was more fear in her face than bewilderment. "Oh no!… No!…"

"My dear, good lady, I did not mean to alarm you." He watched her closely as he spoke: watching was one of his passions. "All I meant was that there was something a little strange, a little—as you say—irregular in the proceeding. There was nothing more to it than that."

As he spoke there was a shout from the floor above, and a man came flying downstairs as fast as he could run.

"Help! Police!" cried the man, stopping at the last stair and swaying against the wall. "Quick! Get the police!"

"The police?"

"Yes, quickly!… Mr Maxwell—he's dead… Murdered!"

Miss Framer screamed shortly and fell forward on to her ledgers. The inkpot she upset at the same time erased the work of a week.

"Come, sir," said Verity sternly to the dishevelled man by the stairs. "A little assistance, if you please."

But the man, whom Verity had recognised immediately as the man on the balcony, merely sank to the floor and began babbling to himself.

As dexterously as he could, Verity raised the phone to his lips with one hand and the Manageress to her feet with the other.

"Just breathe quietly," he told her, "and hold on to the desk till you think you can leave go."

Miss Framer tried hard.

The police at Carrington answered at last, and Verity told the story.

"I'm Jackson," said a stern voice at the other end. "Leave everything just as you found it."

"I didn't find it," said Verity, and rang off.

"Oh, my God!" said the man on the floor. "It's terrible… If only I'd never come here."

"Pull yourself together," Verity commanded, leaving Miss Framer's side to haul him to his feet.

But the man continued to moan.

"I'm finished," he gasped to Verity, as he struggled to catch his breath. "This is the end… I should never have come here… What am I to do?"

"Show me to the body," said Verity crisply. "You stay here, Miss Framer."

"No… I'm quite all right—really I am."

The brilliant morning light streaming through the high doors of the vestibule showed her face grey and trembling under its load of powder. There was an ink-smudge on her forehead. She had evidently had a terrible shock.

"Nevertheless, I think it would be far better if you sat here quietly until the police arrive."

She smiled faintly, and obediently sat down on a high-backed chair against the wall.

Mr Verity turned to the man.

"What is your name, sir?" he asked.

"That's Mr Paxton," said the Manageress dully, as the man himself seemed incapable of answering.

"Well, then, Mr Paxton, be so good as to precede me upstairs."

Mr Paxton goggled, but though his mouth moved, no words came out of it. He was a small man against whose pale face and sand-white hair the jet-black rims of a pair of great spectacles made a startling contrast. At the present moment, with his doll-like head lolling against the wall and his tiny body held from crumpling only by the force of Verity's huge arm, he resembled nothing so much as a trampled puppet.

"We will go," said Verity, turning him round firmly to face the way he had just come. "But first of all, you must hand me that gun I see in your pocket."

Dazedly Paxton took the gun from his pocket and handed it over.

Verity examined it. It was fully loaded, and had not been recently fired.

"Good. Now lead the way, like a sensible man. Oh—and don't forget to point out the sights of interest to me as we pass, will you?"

"What do you mean?" gasped Paxton, reeling before so much action.

"Oh, things like the patch of blood at our feet, for instance."

Paxton looked round wildly.

"Blood?"

"Yes, where you slipped down on the floor." He indicated a dark stain at the foot of the stairs. "There's a certain amount of it on your suit too; that may need explanation a little later on… Come along, my dear sir."

They went upstairs to the first floor. Mr Verity saw a wide corridor flanked down its sides by cream doors with shiny number-plates. Paxton stopped before number 3.

"After you," said Verity politely.

Mr Paxton

Hesitantly the little man turned the handle. But it did not yield. Verity smiled encouragingly.

"Shall we try a little harder?"

"I can't!" cried Paxton peevishly. "It's locked!… Can't you see it's locked?"

He started banging on it.

"Locked?"

Paxton's face was livid as he turned from the door.

"I swear—on my oath, I swear I didn't lock it! Oh, my God!…"

"A key is an easier thing to find than you might suppose," said Verity sternly.

"Oh no—I swear I didn't!… Who are you, anyway?"

The noise of a struggle came from the vestibule below. Miss Framer called out in alarm, and a male voice—a local—cried roughly: "No, yer don't!" Then there was a short scuffle. The detective seized Paxton by the shoulder, and almost tucking him under his arm, set off down the stairs again. In the hall a man of about forty was standing, his arms pinioned behind him by a stocky policeman. Verity noticed a dark stain down the front of his coat: he released Paxton to examine it at closer quarters.

"A novel fashion," he said quietly, comparing the colour with the mark on Paxton's suit. "Nice work, Constable."

"Who the devil are you?" asked the prisoner furiously.

"That is just what Mr Paxton was asking before your arrival! Though I can't think why. I should have thought everyone knew me!" He turned to the constable for confirmation. "Can you think why, Constable?"

The constable agreed that everyone knew Mr Verity hereabouts.

"Verity? The amateur detective?" He tossed his head at the Manageress. "Miss Framer, tell this gentleman who I am. The oaf behind me might care to know too."

"Yes, of course. This is Mr Cunningham, gentlemen. I'm sure there's been a terrible mistake."

"One of your guests?"

"He certainly is. A most respectable gentleman. Believe me, Mr Verity."

Mr Cunningham said nothing, but tried at once to look respectable, injured and indifferent.

"But what," asked Verity, "is he being held for? Surely the constable didn't catch him trying to get in somebody's bedroom too?"

"No, sir," said the constable, impassively. "I caught him coming out."

Miss Framer swayed slightly against the desk. Even Mr Verity found concentration an effort.

"Life among the denizens of Amnestie must be very uneventful," he said at last.

"I'm sure there's been a terrible mistake…" repeated Miss Framer stupidly. "I'm sure there has… really there has…"

Verity bowed to her.

"I'd take your word for almost anything, Miss Framer. May I please borrow your pass-key for a moment?"

"Well, no, I'm afraid—"

"Thank you." He turned to the constable. "You found him climbing out of a window?"

"Yes, sir. Going real fast, 'e was. Came down the drainpipe in no time! Didn't see me waitin' fer 'im till 'e'd got ter the bottom."

"Yet once more the sacrifice of vision to pace," murmured Verity. "The Modern Dilemma seems to crop up everywhere."

Cunningham spat angrily and writhed in his captor's grasp.

"Now look here, Verity. I've stood just about enough of this. I have a perfect right to leave my room any way I please!"

"Yes. Mr Paxton here seems to feel the same about going in. By the way, Constable, permit me to introduce my prisoner to yours. Mr Paxton—Mr Cunningham."

The two men glared at each other in silence. It was clear they had already met.

Miss Framer was rummaging frantically among the things on her desk.

"I'm sorry," she said, with a returning firmness in her voice. "I seem to have lost my pass-key just for the moment. I could have sworn I put it on that hook last night."

"Please don't trouble yourself," said Verity casually. "I didn't really expect it to be there."

"But why...?"

"To facilitate the murder, my dear lady—or prevent its discovery."

"Murder?" The constable's jaw dropped. "Murder?"

"Yes, yes, someone's been killed upstairs. You may deduce a fair amount of blood from the stains on our friends' coats. Inspector Jackson will be here any minute from Carrington. They told me specifically not to touch anything. Come out

Mr Cunningham

into the street with me and see whether we can see them coming. Oh… and do release Mr Cunningham. It's far too late for him to conceal anything now—except perhaps a pass-key, and some of his more controllable reactions."

He wandered out into the bright street, and the policeman followed doubtfully in his wake. The two suspects were left alone in the hall with Miss Framer, who eyed them both uncomprehendingly. White-faced and trembling, the two men fell to a fierce scrutiny of each other.

"An interesting start to the day," said Verity with pleasure. "Tell me, Constable, which window you saw Mr Cunningham come out of."

"That one, sir—the third along from the end, on the left of the drain-pipe. Or no… wait a mo'—p'r'aps it was the one next to it."

Mr Verity's smile left his lips for almost the first time that morning. On the window that Paxton had entered a few minutes earlier there was now a reddish smudge.

"Are you sure you can do no better than that?" he asked anxiously.

"No, sir, to be honest, I can't. I'm pretty sure it's the third one along, but I wouldn't swear to it. I didn't rightly start taking note of 'im till 'e was on the pipe. It might be the fourth."

"And there'll be no finger-prints," said Verity sadly. "I know it in my bones."

"Oughtn't we to go up, sir?" asked the constable nervously.

"When our superiors arrive," the old man replied absently. "Let us enjoy the sunlight while we can."

From the end of the main street a car came speeding towards them, bearing inside Inspector Jackson, a sergeant and three constables: outside the doors of 'The Charter' all that was authoritative in Carrington met all that was enlightened in Amnestie.

CHAPTER II

ON THE ADVICE OF MR VERITY, PAXTON AND CUNNINGHAM were locked up in the dining-room. The two suspects were left sitting at a small table laid for two, with a card reading RESERVED between them and a policeman watching over them. Miss Framer had not yet found her pass-key, and had also begun to cry.

"We have wasted too much time already," said Verity. "It is now imperative we gain access to that room."

"There's always the window," said Jackson, following him upstairs. He was a red-faced man of twenty-nine, nervous and inadequate beside the old man.

"Once set your men tramping through that window, and all clues will be lost forever."

"Well, sir—"

"There's only one thing for it. It's an old lock. We must use Paxton's gun on it."

Before Miss Framer had time to hear about the idea and protest, the lock was shot off and the door itself hurled open. A scene of terrible chaos faced them. The prevailing impression was of blood: blood on the carpet and the rumpled bed, blood on the walls, the curtains and the window-panes. The floor was littered with overturned furniture, clothes, books and papers, a set of golf-clubs, two whisky bottles and a concomitant tooth-mug. Among the debris lay the body, between the door and the great wardrobe which filled the right wall of the room: it was curled over on its face, and still dressed in silk pyjamas—once white, now a streaming scarlet.

"Don't move him till the doctor's seen him," said the Inspector to his sergeant.

"That's in case anyone should feel the need to," added Verity.

No one apparently did. With elaborate care the sergeant and two constables skirted the bright, wet bundle and began their more minute observation of the room.

"There's been quite a struggle," said Jackson superfluously. "Quite a struggle."

"And I was bounding down the hill singing my head off…"

"I beg pardon, sir?"

"Nothing," said Verity, shrugging his shoulders. He was standing by the window, looking down into the street. "You know, this thing is really beginning to intrigue me. I mean it's getting really fascinating."

"I'm afraid I don't follow you, sir," said Jackson stiffly.

Verity smiled.

"Well, a locked door I could just about understand:—but a locked window!…"

"What? It can't be!"

"I'm afraid it is—fully locked on the inside."

Jackson hurried over. Together they contemplated the bloodstained window in dumbfounded silence. Mr Verity, of course, was right.

"When does the doctor arrive?" the old man asked at last.

Inspector Jackson

"I 'phoned the man here," said Jackson briskly. "Thought it would be quicker. He's pretty good."

"Well?"

"He wasn't in, so I left a message with his housekeeper."

"But how long did she say he'd be?"

"Oh, not long. He'd just gone over to Mrs Treacher. I gather she calls him about three times a week."

Jackson smiled for the first time.

"But I don't believe he has. No one ever seems to be sick over here in Amnestie. Dr Pelham says it's the air."

"'Cooks' should issue posters about it," said Verity testily. "'Come to 'Appy Amnestie! WE CURE YOU *AND* KILL YOU!'"

"Yes, sir," said Jackson.

He was down on his hands and knees exploring the carpet, and rather displeased at having permitted himself to play second-fiddle to this blustering old man. It was therefore with obvious pride that he spied the revolver lying in a corner of the room.

"Be careful with that, Matthews: watch out for finger-prints now!"

The find was carefully wrapped in a handkerchief by his impassive sergeant.

Jackson put it to his nose.

"Recently fired," he announced. ".45 Service. Two bullets missing."

"Excellent," said Verity benevolently. "I see your print man is going to be kept pretty busy."

Jackson nodded, and became more efficient in his manner than ever. It did not take his men long to discover the key of the door lying on the carpet nearby. Those of the victim's belongings which Johnson regarded as specially important were carefully wrapped and placed on the desk. They had just started examining the bric-a-brac and papers when a curious moaning and scuffling caught their ears.

"The wardrobe!" said Jackson, moving quickly. "Damn!—it's one of those doors with an automatic lock. You can't open it without a key!"

There was more scuffling, and then a noise as of someone in pain. Finally, as the four men waited in silence, there came very distinctly the sound of a key being fitted into a lock. The handle turned, and the door swung slowly open.

On the floor, her ankles tightly roped together, squatted a girl—a brunette with braided hair. As Jackson noticed, she was pretty. As Verity noticed, she was a waitress.

"I've just got my mouth free, honestly," she said. She held up what looked like a gag, and a rope trailed loosely from her wrists. "It took me ages to get my arms free."

"How long have you been in there?" asked Verity.

"Oh, hours and hours!…" She started crying.

He noticed that her accent was good: a voice always reverts to its native vowel sounds in moments of stress.

"Do you mean that literally?" he asked.

"My head aches…"

"How long have you really been here?"

"Now don't try to talk," said Inspector Jackson kindly. This is advice only given on the screen—where women have occasionally been known to take it.

"Nonsense!" said Verity. "Talk at once! The longer she weeps among the camphor-balls the more fantastic the story she'll tell. What happened to you?... Oh, for heaven's sake get her out of there!"

With great dexterity Jackson lifted her out of the cupboard and carried her from the room without letting her see the late Mr Maxwell, or too much of his blood around the bedroom. Two men were left searching it expertly, and the other constable followed Mr Verity downstairs.

"Why, it's Alice!" cried Miss Framer, rushing forward indignantly. "Is she hurt?"

Miss Framer had evidently conquered her tears, and was her usual, formidable self again.

"No, just frightened," said Jackson reassuringly. "Let me handle this, please."

"Yes, of course, but—"

"Is there anywhere we could be alone a few minutes?"

"In there!" said Miss Framer suspiciously, opening the door of the lounge. "Is that all you want?"

"Yes, thank you—for the moment. I shall want to see you next, if you don't mind."

"I'll be at my desk when you want me," she said crisply.

As he followed the Inspector and the girl into the room, Verity wondered why all such ladies in "good" seaside hotels shared so general and yet so prickly a hostility.

"It's the kind of unlocalised displeasure that goes with amber beads," he murmured aloud.

"I beg pardon, sir?" said the constable, bringing up the rear.

"Just give Inspector Jackson a hand with Alice—there's a good chap."

"I can manage," said Jackson, stiffly setting the bewildered girl on her feet. "There…"

The room was lighter than most rooms of its type: spacious, well-rugged, and containing a great many armchairs in green velvet. In the middle stood a large mahogany table, and around it little satellite tables whose innumerable ash-trays and back copies of the 'Sphere' presumably helped Miss Framer's guests to lounge. Jackson turned to his sergeant.

"We'll make this our headquarters, Matthews. I shall want to see everyone in due course."

"Yes, sir."

"And let me know when they're through upstairs."

"Yes, sir."

"And tell me the minute the doctor arrives," added Verity.

"Very good, sir."

The Inspector crossed to the large table, shifted its potted plant to the end, and sat down.

"Well," he said to Alice, "how do you feel now?"

The girl was sitting on a long wicker settee and dabbing feebly at her head: she was pretty in a hard sort of way, and her face was small and strained. All the time she kept glancing from the red-faced Inspector to the flannelled hulk of Mr Verity behind him. The blue sparks under his tufted brows seemed to be fixed upon her with blazing concentration. Instinctively she turned her head to avoid them, and reluctantly gave her attention to the Inspector.

"You're sure you're well enough to answer questions?" he asked.

Alice Burton

"Oh yes, I'm all right… I'd like to tell you."

"Good." Jackson smiled encouragingly. "Your name is Alice?"

"Yes. Alice Burton."

"You're a waitress here?"

"Yes."

"How long have you been here?"

"Two weeks."

"Good. Did you know Mr Maxwell?"

"Mr…?"

"Mr Maxwell. The man whose death we are concerned with."

The girl opened her mouth abruptly, but made no sound. Her whole attitude expressed the most utter surprise—surprise and, as Verity noted in her attractive eyes, irrepressible relief.

"Syracuse," he said, half to himself.

"What was that, sir?"

"I'll tell you afterwards, Inspector." He strolled over to an occasional table and picked up the first 'Sphere' on the pile.

The poor girl was rather unnerved by now, and began to stammer out a story punctuated by gasps and stifled sobs.

"He called me upstairs, sir—that's the truth, honestly."

"Who called you up?" asked Jackson.

"Mr Maxwell, sir."

"What time was this?"

"About half-past seven."

"Yes?"

"He said he wanted to see me right away. You see… I always took his orders—so of course I had to go."

"What do you mean, you 'took his orders'?"

"Well, sir, Mr Maxwell was a very strange man. He… he always ate his meals by himself—alone in his room. And I… always took them to him."

"Never anybody else?"

"No."

She hesitated, watching him cautiously.

"Wasn't that rather odd?"

"I suppose it was."

"A moment ago you used the expression 'I had to go'. Didn't you like going?"

Miss Burton flushed quickly and lowered her eyes.

"I didn't mind," she said.

Mr Verity beamed behind the pages of his 'Sphere'. He could not have conducted things better himself.

"Go on, please," said Jackson.

"Well, I went up to see what it was he wanted for breakfast. He took quite a time ordering—he always did—and then, when he was nearly done…"

"Yes?" The tone in the Inspector's prompt question discouraged hysterics.

"Then a man came in through the door with a mask over his face!"

"A mask?"

"What did Mr Maxwell order for breakfast?" asked Verity.

"Kidneys and bacon," said Alice. Her voice was trembling.

"Never mind that," Jackson snapped angrily. "This man with the mask—what did he do?"

"He had a gun in his hand, sir, and he told me to put my hands up and go into the corner. Then he and Mr Maxwell started having a terrible row."

"A row? What about?"

"I can't say for certain, sir. I was so frightened I didn't take much notice. It was over money, I think. Oh yes—I remember. The man in the mask said, 'I've paid my last shilling to you, Maxwell.' I remember that."

"Well, then what happened?"

"They started fighting."

"Even though the man held a gun?"

(Inspector Jackson clearly knew his business.)

"Oh yes, sir. Mr Maxwell jumped on him, and they started fighting all round the room. They made a terrible mess. If I hadn't been so frightened I'd have screamed... Then suddenly there was a terrific noise—the gun went off. Mr Maxwell was shot... in the back..."

She started to tremble again. Jackson interposed hastily.

"Yes? And then?"

"And then I fainted. Just before I did, I saw the man in the mask: he had Mr Maxwell in his arms and was pulling him round the room—against the walls and the door—as if he were dancing with him. It was horrible. The blood was beginning to flow fast..."

"And you woke up in the cupboard?"

"Yes. I found the key right beside me, under my hand."

"Remarkable," said Verity.

"You don't believe me, do you?" she said wildly. "You think I killed Mr Maxwell?"

"Why should you want to do that?" asked Verity sweetly. "Because he disapproved of the quality of your breakfasts?"

The girl burst into a flood of tears, and the Inspector intervened kindly.

"You've been through enough for the moment, Miss Burton. I'm sure we can finish this another time, when you feel a little stronger. Locksley! see that Miss Burton gets a cup of something, will you? Then come back here."

"Yes, sir."

With an assured display of regulated tenderness Constable Locksley guided Miss Burton from the room.

"That's interesting," said Jackson thoughtfully. "When I first told her that Maxwell was dead, she looked more than surprised. Perhaps she was just acting, and then realised it didn't square with the story she was going to tell."

"I'd trust the look rather than the story," said Verity, laying down his magazine. "That is, if the two were incompatible."

"You mean she was really surprised to hear that Maxwell was dead?"

"No, but I fancy she hated him so much that she still can't quite accept the idea of his death. The look we saw on her face was unquestionably one of relief. Relief that what could have been only a dream was in fact true."

"Maybe."

"I've seen that look once before on the marble face of a head I dug up near Syracuse. I think it was the braided hair that reminded me. There is a moral quality about that smile—the kind of triumphant pleasure which must have illumined the faces of the God-ridden in ancient Greece, when they witnessed the purging of iniquity. Only toned down, of course, because this is Amnestie and not Athens."

"It sounds like a description of insanity to me," said Jackson.

"Oh, I daresay." He sat down heavily and lit one of his little Cuban cigars. "I am not discussing Miss Burton's sanity. Like everything else in this business, it has yet to be proved. Of course, she's not really a waitress—but that, if anything, is a point in her favour."

"I agree with you there. She clearly hasn't been a waitress all her life. The accent's wrong. Let's have Miss Framer in: perhaps she can throw some light on things."

"Collecting statues is a useful occupation," said Verity, as they waited for P.C. Locksley to return. "It sets you observing people's expressions with greater attention. Teaches you to watch out for flaws, too."

The constable came back.

"Just ask Miss Framer to step inside, will you?" asked Jackson. "And then tell Matthews I want that gun we found, right away."

"There are a few people alive today," Verity continued, "who deserve to have their faces sculpted in marble. Miss Burton is one of them. As for the rest of my pretty large acquaintance: some deserve stone, many more terracotta— and by far the great majority, putty."

Miss Framer came into the room.

"See what I mean?" he added.

"Sit down, Miss Framer," said Jackson politely.

"I think," she said, thrusting a shapeless mauve skirt at him, "that Mr Verity will be glad to receive this."

"Ah, my bathing-costume! I had quite forgotten it! That is very considerate of you, Miss Framer. I will not, however, be bathing whilst there is matter more attractive here to hold me."

Miss Framer looked shocked, and sat down slowly.

"To the police," she said, "this sort of thing must constitute a most interesting diversion. You cannot expect me to view it in the same way."

"No, of course not. I—"

"When news of what has occurred here appears in the newspapers, I shall be absolutely ruined."

"As I remember it," said Verity politely, "'The Charter' of Amnestie has appeared more than once in the newspapers already."

"That was before my time," said Miss Framer quickly. "I can assure you that nothing like that has occurred since I was put in charge."

"I can well believe that," the old man smiled.

"But something like this—a murder!"

"How well did you know Mr Maxwell?" asked Jackson suddenly.

Miss Framer looked uncomfortable for a moment. Then she squared her shoulders and, sitting upright, faced her questioner across the table. Here, she realised, began the cross-examination.

"Hardly at all. He had only been with us five days."

"You mean he came last Friday?"

"That is so."

"Was he a very—eccentric gentleman?"

"I'm afraid he was. He took all his meals in his rooms, and hardly went out except at night. He told me he worked at night."

"A description which has opened the trial of every cat-burglar I ever attended," said Verity, watching Miss Framer carefully.

"I'm sure I'm not implying any such thing," she said hastily.

"No, but all the same the thought of burglary was not so very far from your mind earlier this morning. When I told you about the man on the balcony climbing in through a window, you were very frightened. I was observing you."

"I?"

"Or was it something else?"

"I don't understand…"

"What do you know of the relationship between Mr Paxton and Mr Maxwell? Or Mr Cunningham and Mr Maxwell?"

"Relationship?"

"Oh, come now!" Mr Verity, who had firmly taken over from Jackson, leaned forward and twinkled at her. "Try to be more explicit."

"But Mr Cunningham only came last night."

"Still, he did meet Mr Maxwell?"

"Yes, he did."

"Well?"

"They did not appear to like each other. In fact, if I might say so without prejudice to Mr Cunningham, he seemed to take great dislike to Mr Maxwell. Yes, a real dislike…"

"I see. What time did Mr Cunningham arrive last night?"

"About nine o'clock, I think it was."

"And Mr Paxton?"

"Oh, he's been here since Monday."

There was a knock at the door, and Sergeant Matthews brought in the gun, still wrapped in a handkerchief.

"Two bullets fired, sir."

"Good."

"And Dr Pelham's just come, sir."

"Excellent," said Jackson. "Take him upstairs. Tell him we'll be with him in a minute."

"Yes, sir."

"Where is Miss Burton?" asked Verity.

"In the kitchen, sir, having a cup of tea. Constable Locksley's with her."

"Excellent."

"That's all, Matthews." Jackson turned to Miss Framer, who was breathing heavily. "How long has Miss Burton been in your employment?"

"About a fortnight, Inspector. I can give you the exact date if you want it."

"Do you find she's a reliable girl?"

"Yes, on the whole. We've only had one complaint."

"Oh? What was that?"

"That she kept her thumbs in among the vegetables as she served them."

"Thank you. You were saying that Mr Paxton has been here since Monday. Did he and Mr Maxwell know each other?"

Miss Framer did not reply for a moment. Then she said:

"Yes. They knew each other slightly. One evening they met on the stairs, just as Mr Maxwell was going out."

"The meeting was—cordial?"

"Oh yes, very cordial!" She nodded vigorously. "They just talked for a few minutes, and then Mr Maxwell left. Very cordial, I should say."

"That's most interesting. Now there's just one more thing, and then you can go."

He unwrapped the handkerchief and laid the gun on the desk. It was a heavy Service revolver, with a pearl handle.

"Have you ever seen this before?"

Miss Framer betrayed at once that she had.

"Why—yes."

"When?"

"Last night. It fell out of Mr Cunningham's coat pocket as he took it off in the vestibule."

"Are you sure?"

"Positive. I didn't like the look of it at all."

"Hence the fright this morning," said Verity.

"Oh no—"

"Why didn't you inform me?" asked Jackson severely.

"Between you," she retorted angrily, "you haven't given me the chance."

"Quite true," said Verity cheerfully. "Miss Framer, how many short-term guests are there here?"

"Mr Paxton and Mr Cunningham are the only ones at the moment. Oh, and Mr Tudor."

"Who on earth is that?"

"A very strange gentleman indeed. He arrived two weeks ago."

"About the same time as Miss Burton?"

"Yes! I'm afraid you'll have to speak to him yourself, because I can't make any sense of him."

"Is he dangerous?"

"I shouldn't be surprised. He calls himself King Richard the Fourth."

"Better and better!" cried Verity, chuckling and rubbing his hands. "A corpse in a blood-soaked room; a locked door and a locked window; a masked man; a beautiful girl trussed inside a wardrobe; and now a pretender to the throne! This is superb!"

Miss Framer looked at him with frost in her eyes. She turned to Jackson.

"While I seem to be amusing Mr Verity," she said, "I am still very busy. If you have finished with me, there are a great many things that need my attention."

Jackson nodded.

"Yes, thank you: that'll be all for the moment. I'll send for you should I want you again. Oh—and no one is to leave here,—not even long-term residents."

"Very good."

"And I know we can rely on your co-operation, Miss Framer."

She looked surprised, but only rose and walked quickly out of the room.

Matthews came in almost immediately, carrying a sheaf of papers in his hand, which he laid before Jackson.

"These were in his desk, sir. Right at the back."

Verity rose, extended his eye-glass ("I always need it for handwriting") and looked over the first of the pile.

'*My dear Paxton*', it read, '*this is the last time you'll be hearing from me for at least a month, so why not celebrate my going away? Shall we say £200? Same arrangements. M.*'

"I think," said Mr Verity slowly, "that we shall need everybody's finger-prints. The tea-cups are easiest. Tell Locksley to start with Miss Burton down in the kitchen. Prevent her from washing up."

"Look here, sir, is that quite the thing?" Jackson was clearly shocked.

"No," said Verity smilingly. "It isn't. But when you have an imitation waitress telling an absurd story about masked men—a story that could have come straight from the pages of a novelette—well, it's best to check up. Insults to one's intelligence aren't the thing, either."

"I see what you mean."

"In any case, my real object here is Paxton. The fact that he didn't fire his own gun makes it all the more possible that he did fire Cunningham's.

"It's as I said: your finger-print men are going to be kept very, very busy."

CHAPTER III

D R PELHAM WAS A SHORT, WRY, FASTIDIOUS PERSON; he wore a pince-nez, and showed the gold in his teeth whenever he laughed at his own jokes, which was often. He stood now in the sunny garden of the hotel, talking excitedly to Verity and Jackson, the while he explored a hunch-backed apple-tree with a stick for any fruit that might have ripened early.

"Oh yes, I've seen him," he was saying. "He'll have to be moved, of course. I can't examine him properly up there. I should say he died between 6.30 and 8.30. Obviously shot in the back. Just what happened there I don't know. He got two bullets in him."

"Yes," said Jackson. "There are two missing from the revolver."

"But whether one or both killed him—for what it's worth—I can't say at the moment."

"Did you know him yourself, Doctor?" asked Verity.

"Oh, indeed, yes. If ever a man deserved a couple of bullets, he did."

"Really?"

"Oh, just squab and beastly."

"Squab?"

"Sweating with money, too." Dr Pelham spat out his bite of green apple. "And sly. The kind of man who'd make life a Puritan hell for his children and spend his mornings tickling the secretary. By the way, did he have any children?"

"The police are finding out everything they can," said Jackson. "No family has been traced, as yet"—(it was now noon)—"and there are no family letters among his papers."

"Ah! His papers!" The doctor put his head on one side and looked at the Inspector wistfully. "How I'd like to settle down with those for a cosy evening's reading! I do envy you detectives—especially you private ones."

"I am sensible of it," said Verity, lighting one of his little cigars. "I started life with a very genuine zeal for the public good. It was my highest ideal to give devoted service in some work of reform. I had, in fact, a positive lust for amelioration. Yet it was only when I had discovered how to make my improving society dependent on a much deeper desire to wash its dirty linen in private, that I became a detective. After that, I was a much more likeable person. How did you know Mr Maxwell, Doctor?"

"I met him several times in the streets. Mostly at night."

"Ah yes, he always walked at night, did he not?"

"Either walked or was driven."

"Driven?"

"Yes, the taxi-driver here, a very decent young man, used to drive him around in the small hours. He suffered terribly from insomnia: so do I—though I fancy mine is not provoked by the same sort of guilty conscience. We often met. He maintained that driving round aimlessly at night was good for him. It was *his* money of course."

"Technically," said Verity. "Well, Doctor, we'll see you later. What about dinner tonight? Come over at 8.30."

"I'll be glad to," said the little man, shouldering his walking-stick. "It's very good of you, to be sure. In the meantime I'll be taking a closer look at our friend."

Verity and Jackson stepped back through the French window into the lounge.

"An admirable man," said Verity. "It's a pleasure to work with a man who's on the same side as I am."

"And which side is that?" asked Jackson wearily.

"The murderer's. Dr Pelham has already confirmed me in my instinctive detestation of Mr Maxwell... However—to work! We must still catch our man while the trail is hot. Each man hangs the thing he loves!"

Jackson stared at him heavily.

"Shall we go through the papers now?" he asked.

"Excellent idea, Jackson. Most of them seem irrelevant, but we'll examine the lot, just in case. Give me half, and we should be finished in thirty minutes. Where, by the way, are our two prize suspects?"

"Still in the dining-room, where I put them."

"Good. I suggest you see them presently."

As the doctor had predicted, the papers of the late Mr Maxwell made fascinating reading. They were mostly in the same vein as his note to Paxton, and among them Jackson discovered a draft letter to Cunningham. Apart from these, there were accounts of sums received from his victims, some of them neatly pencilled on the backs of despairing letters from men and women who could pay no longer—or who said they couldn't.

Among these letters addressed to Maxwell was one which caught the eye of Verity and kindled in it the light of battle.

"Listen to this!" he shouted, screwing in his eye-glass with a gesture. "'*Maxwell: Alice has told me everything. This is the end of the line for you. Just you try to see her once more and see what you get. Just once more, Maxwell, and you're a goner.*' It's signed '*Winnidge*'."

"Is it dated?"

"The postmark's indistinct. It looks like sometime last month."

"Where was it posted?"

"Here—in Amnestie."

"Winnidge, you say?"

"Yes, do you know him?"

"No, but it looks as if we have another good suspect."

"The more the merrier! When the number of suspects is continually increasing, and the number of corpses remains constant, you get a sort of inflation. The value of your individual suspect, of course, becomes hopelessly depreciated. That, for your real detective, is a state of paradise."

"Shall we have one of them in?" Jackson asked quietly.

"Of course! At once!"

The Inspector opened the door and spoke to Locksley.

"Send Mr Paxton in, and relieve Matthews upstairs. Tell him to get some lunch. And let me know the moment the print-men arrive."

Paxton came into the lounge. He had pulled himself together somewhat since Mr Verity had pulled him upstairs four hours before.

"Sit down, please," said Jackson. "I want to ask you a few questions."

Mr Paxton sat down, glaring through his great spectacles.

"Let me see, it was you who gave the alarm, wasn't it?"

"Yes."

"Will you tell me, in your own words, what happened?"

Paxton shifted nervously in his seat and then, with extreme reluctance, began.

"It was like this. I went to see Maxwell in his room."

"What time was this?"

"About ten to eight."

"How did you get in?" asked Verity.

"Through the window."

"The window?"

"Yes. I—I didn't want to be seen entering."

"Why ever not?"

"Well, you see—I did not want anyone to know I knew him… That is—" He stopped aghast. "I'm afraid I'm expressing myself badly. What I mean is, people might have wondered what I was doing—"

"Indeed they might," assented Verity.

"You were armed, of course?" asked Jackson.

"Yes."

Verity smiled.

"I'm afraid we have your gun. We'll return it to you, of course—after the arrest. Was it new?"

"Yes."

"Where did you buy it?"

"At Jessop's in the Strand. I said I wanted it for personal protection…"

"I see. That explains why you got an Army Service revolver.

Curious this fondness for .45's. One would almost think some kind of league had been formed to kill this man."

"That isn't funny to me!"

A flash of anger showed in Paxton's eyes. Then suddenly he began moaning again, as he had done at the bottom of the stairs. Once again, too, the resemblance to a smashed puppet reappeared.

"I swear I didn't do it!…" he said, more to himself than anyone else. "Appearances are against me… So? What does that matter? I didn't do it… They know I didn't…"

"How many bullets did you buy with it?" asked Verity firmly.

"Six… Oh, I know you think I did it. I don't care! I meant to do it. I bought the gun to do it! I'm sorry I didn't. I tell you, I'm sorry I didn't!"

"You mean you found yourself forestalled?"

"Of course I did! Someone had been there before me. That's why I called for help." He turned to Verity. "You know I did that."

"Louis Tissier, railway-worker of Lyons, smashed his wife's head with a fish-plate, then informed his neighbours, sent for the police, and phoned his mother-in-law."

"No one has levelled any accusations yet," said Jackson imperturbably. "What we want is the truth."

"And I'm giving it to you! I went there to talk to him—to reason with him!…"

"And if he wouldn't listen?"

Jackson waited about ten seconds for the expected answer.

"To kill him. You see… I could stand it no longer. Listen! It happened years ago, when I first started practising law."

"You are a solicitor?"

"I qualified in 1924. I worked in London—did quite well, too... I didn't really need the money."

"What was it you did?"

There was an even longer pause before, staring hard at the carpet, Mr Paxton confessed in a whisper:

"I cooked an alibi... for a friend. A lady. It was a dreadful thing to do, of course—but I felt sorry for her. She was very helpless..."

"And evidence of this got into Maxwell's hands?"

"I must have been mad..."

"And then?"

"For years he used it against me. In the end my nerves got so bad—I had to give up practice."

"What did you do then?"

"Oh, this and that. What I could... this and that... Oh, God, I hated him!..." The tears began rolling down his face. "There was no reason... he didn't know me—it didn't matter to him. There was no reason, don't you see? But he was like that!..."

Jackson averted his gaze.

"And he still went on even after you had given up practice?"

"He smashed my whole life. It took him just over two years. I would have killed him a hundred times over!... I would... but I didn't!... I swear I didn't!"

He began sobbing helplessly, looking so much like a broken doll expressing resentment at its relegation to the playbox, that Jackson rose and put a hand on his shoulder.

"That'll do for the moment, Mr Paxton. Go and get some food. I'll see you a little later."

He smiled encouragingly as he helped him up.

As the little man turned to go, Mr Verity leaned forward in his chair.

"Just one thing, Mr Paxton. Did you lock the window when you went into Maxwell's room?"

Paxton shook his head firmly in the negative, and groped his way out still weeping to himself.

"God, this Maxwell was a swine!" said Jackson after a pause.

"It's as I said before," observed Verity. "It's hardly a pleasure being on the side of the Law."

A tall, proud man, with raven locks flowing over his high, white forehead, stood surveying them at the French window. He was dressed in a long, dark suit, and a shirt whose frayed collar and cuffs encased a prickly neck and a pair of heavy wrists.

"Pleasure?" he boomed at them. "Pleasure? It's a duty! Provided it *is* the Law!"

"Who are you?" asked Verity, surprised.

"My name is Richard Tudor. If the Law held any sway in England, I should be her rightful king."

"Come in," said Verity, smiling politely. "Take a seat."

"I am accustomed to people remaining seated when I come into a room," said the tall man loftily. "I suppose it is only to be expected."

"We are very busy, sir, if you don't mind," said Jackson firmly.

"I am used to that kind of talk, too, young man. But what else is to be expected from a People which has for generations paid public allegiance to usurpers?"

Richard Tudor

"A readiness to be imposed upon, I should imagine," said Verity, lighting another cigar. "From whom do you claim descent?"

"From His Majesty King Edward the Sixth, son of King Henry the Eighth!"

"Under your correction, Mr Tudor, I have always thought that His Majesty King Edward the Sixth died at the age of fifteen—unmarried. The Virgin King, in fact."

"False! Quite false!" Mr Tudor came much nearer and laid a hand on his arm with sinister emphasis. "You must understand," he said, "that my noble ancestor knew the tremors of love!"

"At fifteen?"

"No, at fourteen. He was, of course, precocious—like all his family. The trouble was that the girl of his choice was a Catholic."

"I always believed that Edward—your noble ancestor—was a devoted patron of the English Reformation."

"That is true, of course—before his marriage. But" (he nodded intimately, and drew even nearer) "there are some things even more persuasive to a young boy than religion." Mr Verity looked surprised. "However, there was one person who could not afford to have this known—one person whose position as real ruler of England depended absolutely on the Protestant faction. That man was the Duke of Northumberland—the man who murdered Edward."

"What?"

"Yes, I can prove it!"

"The power behind the throne killed the man on the

throne? Curious! But tell me," asked Verity, dabbing at his ear, "who was this girl you speak of?"

"Her name was Katerina. She came with an embassy from the Court of Spain. She was, in fact, a distant relation of Philip the Second." He preened himself and took a few steps back, the better to narrate his story. "Yes, her secret marriage to Edward was to become a favourite topic of conversation between Philip and Mary later on. I have documents to prove this."

"He married at fourteen?"

"In the greatest of secrecy, of course—surrounded by only a few trusted Lords."

"But surely the King of England wouldn't marry in this manner? Why didn't he come straight out and dare Northumberland to do his worst?"

"What could a boy of fourteen do against a man like the Duke?" (Inspector Jackson indicated with a gesture of impatience that he really couldn't think.) "After all, he did manage to get his young wife and her baby smuggled out of the palace, disguised as the last two stragglers from a popular uprising which had recently been repulsed. I have documents to prove this."

"Nevertheless," Verity purred, "as I remember it, Edward continued to champion the Reformation till the day of his death."

Tudor bridled.

"I have documents to prove this was all a pretence. In private he abjured this new-fangled faith and adhered to the creed of his fathers—I mean of his father."

"May I ask, in light of this complication, what faith you yourself profess?"

"I am an Henrican Catholic," said Mr Tudor loftily.

"That must be difficult for you."

Jackson shifted in his chair. "I'm afraid you'll have to excuse me now. I happen to be very busy."

"I, too, regrettably enough," said Verity, rising. "But do tell me the rest of the story sometime."

"I shall be happy to give you audience," he said, bright-eyed. "Make no mistake, gentlemen. I am Richard the Fourth, King of England—and I have documents to prove it." Then, in a calmer voice, he added: "Continue your work."

He bowed stiffly, turned and strode into the garden.

"Extraordinary," said Verity, thoughtfully.

"Yes!" said Jackson. He was plainly annoyed. "Dr Pelham would doubtless put it down to the air."

CHAPTER IV

"**D**ID YOU NOTICE THE DARK STAIN ON PAXTON'S suit?" asked Jackson when they had recovered themselves.

"Yes. I saw it earlier on. There is also one on Cunningham's coat, and another on the carpet in the vestibule, at the foot of the stairs."

"Yes, I'd been wondering about that."

"Well, the one on the floor doesn't tally with the others, at any rate. The stain on Paxton's coat was new when I saw it. That on the floor was already quite old when he flopped down on it. But I'm pretty sure it's blood in all three cases— and blood from the same body."

"Yes. This gets more difficult every minute."

"You're right, my boy, it does. Of course, I *may* be wrong about the same body: there is always the possibility that the number of corpses is as unstable as the number of suspects. Have you heard of any notabilities disappearing from Amnestie?"

"No, thank God!"

Mr Verity walked up and down the lounge, puffing expansively. One or two elderly and bewildered guests peered in through the French window: the old man bowed to them affably, and they resumed their shamble round the walled garden. The smell of sea and sunbeams reached him, and faint, scrannel chatter. There was mercifully no sign of Mr Tudor.

"By the way," he said, "I see we've neglected something in the Maxwell papers."

He flourished them at the Inspector, who still sat frowning at the table.

"What's that?"

"There's a Memo here to '*see Miss F.*' And it's dated after Maxwell arrived here."

"Miss F.? I wonder—No, it couldn't be…"

"Miss Framer?"

"No one could have anything on her."

His voice was pleading.

"I wouldn't be so sure. I dare say even she sowed a little crop of wild oats once upon a time. It is interesting, too, that she called the meeting of Paxton and Maxwell on the stairs 'very cordial'. From what we have just seen, I should say that was a deliberate lie."

"It certainly looks like it."

"I wonder whether her original 'mistake'—if any—was perjury…"

Jackson lit a cigarette.

"The deeper we go, the more people seem to be involved," he said.

"Precisely. The detective's paradise!"

More guests passed the window.

"We'll have to question them all," said Jackson, without enthusiasm.

"All except King Richard. Unless Maxwell was instrumental in getting him locked up at one period in his life…"

"I wouldn't be surprised at anything now. Shall we have Cunningham in?"

"As you please. I think he will give you a tougher session than Paxton."

Sergeant Matthews came in to report that the print-men had just arrived.

"Good," said Jackson, with as much briskness as he could summon. "Have you had lunch?"

"Yes, sir. Thank you, sir."

"I want to see Mr Cunningham."

"He's waiting outside, sir. And I thought you'd like to know, sir—"

"Yes?"

"When he stood up in the dining-room to come in here, the constable found this under his chair."

He handed over what was obviously Miss Framer's pass-key.

"On the floor under his chair? Are you sure?"

"Positive, sir."

"Right. Get it identified by Miss Framer, and then hand it straight over to the print-men. I've got the gun for them, too, once I've seen Cunningham. Send him in, will you?"

Cunningham came in slowly, sidling round the door and keeping to the walls as much as possible. He seemed afraid to come out into the open spaces of the room, and when he did approach the table it was in two short, ill-considered rushes. This was the first time that Verity had really looked at him. He was an untidy man, ill-kempt and rather dirty.

His face was lean and mottled and wore a sly look. Yet his eyes were quite still—liquid, grey eyes, remote and detached in a cunning face. They seemed quite out of focus, and the effect was unpleasant—as if a really sharp rake-off man had suddenly been struck blind in the middle of a deal. The effort of concentration seemed difficult; the need for it imperative. The conflict showed harshly in this wretched face.

"Good morning," he said, pulling a struggling moustache. "You wanted to see me?"

His voice, now in repose, was far softer and more querulous than the early morning's passion had led Mr Verity to believe.

"Yes," said the Inspector. "I have one or two questions to ask you."

"I'll do my best, Inspector. May I sit down?"

"Please do."

Verity watched in silence.

"You knew Mr Maxwell?" asked Jackson.

"No."

"Oh… You didn't know him at all? Never had any business with him?"

"No. None whatever."

"Yet you were in his room this morning."

"Who—me?"

"The constable who arrested you watched you climb out of his window. Have you forgotten?"

Cunningham smiled vaguely.

"If I overheard him aright this morning, the constable could not for sure identify which window I came out of. I was actually on the drain-pipe before he saw me. It could equally well have been the window next door."

"Mr Paxton's?"

"Yes, Mr Paxton's."

He said this with an air of almost childish pride.

"Or even the one on the other side of Maxwell's?" asked Verity.

"Yes, even that!"

"Because, after all, you did have the pass-key."

"I?… No! Never!… I never had the pass-key!"

"Never?"

Verity looked shocked, and reaching over the table, revealed the revolver in its handkerchief. Cunningham followed him with his eyes.

"Now you had better be very careful," the old man said, "that a fourth lie does not reveal the falsity of your other three. Have you ever seen this before?"

"I—"

He fell silent and appeared to be making a great effort at concentration.

"I'm asking you about this gun," said Verity. "Perhaps I should warn you that it has already been identified by the Manageress as belonging to you."

"That bitch!" He spat furiously with a sudden return to his manner of the morning. "She *would* say that! Can't you see she's covering up for Paxton?"

"Oh? Why should she do that?"

Verity sat strewing innocence before him with a blandishing hand.

"Why? How the devil should I know why? Anyone can see there's something between them... Always together whispering... Always together!..."

"Always? I thought you only arrived last night?"

"I... I did."

Verity rose.

"Mr Cunningham, you are the most wretched liar I have ever met. If I excuse you, it is only because you have too much dope inside you to allow you to be a good one. Once, I imagine, you took smaller doses: at the moment it would not be worth anyone's while to blackmail you about a feature of your life which is obvious to all. Your eyes betray you. Your hands betray you. Above all, to me, your feeble attempts to defend yourself betray you. If you had only realised what a hopeless, irredeemable dope-addict you look, you would not have gone on paying hush-money for so long. And you certainly would not have resorted to violence."

Cunningham looked helplessly up at him, as the vast man swung round the room ejaculating finely at the walls. Jackson sat impassively at his table, but listening with great respect.

"What were you," demanded Verity, "before you started taking the stuff?"

"I worked for a firm of brokers. They fired me."

"Earlier on you told me four lies. The first was when you denied knowing Maxwell; the second when you denied coming out of his window; the third when you denied having the pass-key; the last when you denied, by implication, owning the gun. The letter I have now, and the finger-prints I shall have presently, will tell me all I need to know. Now, when did you buy this Service revolver?"

"I don't understand."

"Come, Mr Cunningham. It has its maker's name inlaid in the handle. Everyone knows Jessop's in the Strand—identification is the easiest thing imaginable."

For a moment Cunningham said nothing. Then:

"Yesterday morning."

"Good," said Verity, and sat down again.

Jackson took up the examination.

"What kind of bullets did you buy?"

"I left that to Mr Jessop," he said cautiously. "I don't know what he chose."

"What reason did you give him for wanting the weapon?"

"I said I was going out East."

"And you needed it for personal protection?"

Cunningham looked startled.

"If he had been wise he'd have given you spray-guns," put in Verity—"both you and Paxton!"

"I have a licence," said Cunningham doggedly.

"We'll require to see it in due course. Now about you and Mr Maxwell——"

"Oh, stop playing with me!" the man broke out. "So you have one of his letters. So you can see it all for yourselves—well, what of it? I had good reason to kill Maxwell! So had everyone who knew him. So had Paxton! Even I know that much... So had that waitress..."

"What waitress?" asked Verity with quiet deliberation.

There was a slight pause. Inspector Jackson looked up sharply from his notes.

"The—the girl I saw go into his room last night. The one Miss Framer calls Alice…"

His voice faltered.

"Yes?"

"I heard them quarrelling—she and Maxwell."

"You heard them last night?"

"Yes. I tell you, everyone who knew him hated him!"

"But not everyone who knew him left their guns in his room."

"I know—that's what I was going to tell you. You see, I lost my gun last night. It was taken from my room. I missed it when I went upstairs after supper."

"What time was that?" asked Jackson.

"Between nine-thirty and ten. I had late supper when I arrived."

"But how could anybody know you had a gun?"

"Miss Framer knew about it. It fell out of my overcoat pocket last night in the hall. She saw it. I know she did!"

He stared Jackson in the face, almost triumphantly.

"Anybody else?" asked the Inspector.

"She could have told Paxton, couldn't she?… She probably did!"

"What evidence have you," asked Jackson judicially, "for saying that Miss Framer knows Mr Paxton as anything more than a guest?"

Cunningham nodded sagely.

"Twice last night I saw them whispering together. Once

in the hall, and once in the corridor outside my room. Whispering, I tell you... Not talking like ordinary people."

"Where is your room?"

"The first floor—on the other side of the hotel. It over-looks the garden."

"Now about this pass-key. When did you take it?"

The furious again succeeded the confidential in Cunningham's manner.

"I tell you I didn't touch it!" he cried, slapping his hand down on the desk. "I've never seen your blasted pass-key!"

"It was found under your chair in the dining-room but a minute ago."

"You're a liar!"

Jackson said nothing.

"It's a plant, then! That's what it is!..." He faced them both wildly. "I never had the key!... If I'd had it—would I hide it there, under my chair? Of all the damn silly places!... I tell you Paxton put it there! He got it from that woman!"

"That's not true," said Verity evenly. "If Paxton had the key, he'd have used it. As it was, he entered Maxwell's room by the window."

Cunningham gaped. "Oh... yes," he said. "Yes."

"Paxton confessed he went to see Maxwell," said Verity quietly. "Why don't you do the same? I know you did."

There was another pause. Finally Cunningham said: "All right. I'll tell you." He was looking at Verity with a sort of fear in his eyes. "I did go."

"I know you did. It's getting late, and you could have spared us the prelude."

"But I didn't have the pass-key, and I didn't have the gun. I went to reason with him—that's all."

"Yes, of course. To reason with him," Verity repeated, wondering how often he had heard the absurd inaccuracy during all his years of detective work. "What form did the reasoning take?"

"I went into the room. It was in a terrible mess. Everything was lying about the room—covered with blood. It was horrible. Maxwell was lying on the floor. He was dead. I know he was dead because I took a closer look. That's when I must have got his blood on my coat. I suppose my gun must have been lying near him too—but I didn't see it. I was panic-stricken—what could I do? I was desperate: no one would believe me if I told them the truth. I can see you don't now—"

"What happened next?"

"I heard a noise in the corridor. Someone was approaching—if he came in, he'd think I did it! No, there were more than one, several people... at any rate I couldn't go out that way... And I couldn't lock the door—"

"You couldn't?"

"There was no key in it."

"I see."

"There was only one thing I could do."

"The window?"

"Yes. I climbed out onto the balcony."

"Then down the drain-pipe into the arms of the constable?"

"Yes. That's the whole story, I swear it."

"It may," conceded Verity, "be a fragment of the truth."

"You're sure there was no one in the room beside Maxwell?" asked Jackson.

"I don't know. I was too frightened to notice... There could have been."

"I see." The Inspector pursed his lips and frowned. "Is that all you can tell us?"

"Yes, that's everything!"

"Just being the last person to see a man alive isn't all that heinous an offence, Mr Cunningham," said Verity.

"I was frightened..." he mumbled again.

"Then you must learn to cast out fear."

"I think that'll be all for the moment," said Jackson, who was now wanting his lunch badly. "I shall be seeing you again, of course, later on. In the meantime I'm afraid that neither you nor Mr Paxton will be allowed to leave the hotel."

"No... I understand," said Cunningham, rising and making for the door. "Of course I understand."

"Nor Miss Burton, nor Miss Framer," added Verity when Cunningham had left the room. "In a way, I'm glad I'm not sleeping here."

Jackson smiled. "All the same, we haven't done a bad morning's work, sir."

"True," said Verity. "We have met a dope-addict, a crook-solicitor, and the girl with the feeblest imagination in Sussex."

"I must admit, it's the tallest story *I've* ever heard."

"*And* Mr Richard Tudor. I have the most pleasing feeling that he doesn't fit into this at all... Oh, by the way, you are coming along to dinner with Dr Pelham tonight?"

"That's very kind of you, sir."

"So I must leave you and lay in provisions. We'll try to sort some of it out tonight."

Jackson looked surprised, but only said: "Are you staying here for lunch?"

"Oh, dear me, no!" Verity heaved himself to his feet. "A plate of Amnestie shrimps on top of three cigars would probably finish me off. By the way, do you know Detective Inspector Rambler?"

"No, sir, I can't say I do."

"He's a Yard man."

"Oh, yes?" Inspector Jackson's manner became a little colder.

"You'll meet him tonight."

"Why, is he staying with you?"

"He will be," said Verity. Then he added, quickly: "There's no question of credit-stealing here. You, of course, will get it all. But the case offers complications which I do not think you have realised. I shall try to point some of them out tonight."

"Yes, sir."

"Now Rambler is an old hand—or rather, an old brain— of very great standing. At the moment he's on holiday, but it might be as well if I put things before him. Tonight is an excellent time—none better. And the sense of being on the inside of things will please Dr Pelham enormously!"

"Yes," said Inspector Jackson thoughtfully. "If you really think that's the best course…"

"I do," said Mr Verity smartly. "Unquestionably the best."

He picked up his mauve bathing suit and strode off to the telephone.

CHAPTER V

THE ARRIVAL OF DETECTIVE INSPECTOR RAMBLER THAT same evening sufficed to dispel all Jackson's suspicions. Though he would not have admitted it to anyone, he was by no means loth to accept help in a case that was rapidly becoming far too much for him to handle alone.

Rambler was on his vacation at the time: this constituted to him the busman's holiday dear to experts and connoisseurs. And, as Verity had briefly explained, the Maxwell case was very much a specimen for the connoisseur.

Rambler was a stout man—as stout as Verity himself: a great, sad-faced hulk with a heavy, pink jowl and a cold, fierce brain. He was curiously named: inaccurately, if one considered his tenacious mind which, once it had seized on a thing, never relaxed its hold till it had thoroughly done with it. He was, as Verity observed of him, "a humourless, single-minded porpoise". Yet anyone who considered his ill-clothed frame, his shirts (always too wide at the neck), and his ties (always too loose at the knot), would agree that the name, with its ability to create a slightly false impression, was still partially appropriate.

He had known Verity well of old, and had solved two of his most formidable cases solely because of the older man's

Inspector Rambler

violent intervention: their association had made both famous, and the talk of the Yard. Verity respected the tamed logic in Rambler; Rambler the explosive vision in Verity. Both shared in common an immense bulk, a healthy appetite for the bizarre, and an absence of friends. Their differences were only such as could not be helped. Verity had a temper and a beard; but Rambler was a professional and could afford neither.

He sat now opposite his host in the long living-room at 'Persepolis' eating the excellent dinner prepared by Verity's housekeeper. As he sat, he swelled gently inside his hacking-jacket, and from time to time fingered his huge, pink jowl. To his right sat Dr Pelham, active and intelligent; and to his left Inspector Jackson, silent—though not peeved—and redder than ever in a smartened uniform.

Night had fallen. The light of a dozen candles fell on the table, and on the faces of the ancient statues grouped around it. Innumerable marble eyes, as shiny and blank as pigeons' eggs, glared down at them from under the frozen ledges of their brows. Verity as usual was talking. The candlelight stained his wide old face and set his eyes afire.

"There have been one or two men," he was saying, "I have met in my lifetime whom I felt I should never understand. No—not even if I devoted many years to it. One was a Sicilian who worked in the garden of my villa outside Naples. It was many years ago. I had unearthed and set up a most delicate little statue—a Priapus in clay. He was really delightful: a fat, laughing, rollicking little handful of terracotta. It made you happy just to gaze at him. Now my gardener hated that statue. Hated it, I firmly believe, for the joy in its grin, and the wrinkles round its little hands and feet. One morning he waited till he thought I was out; then he took his spade and smashed it. Just smashed it! And then buried the pieces among the laurel bushes… I shall never forget that: it made me very frightened."

No one said anything. Mr Verity passed round the wine and the statues flared in the yellow light.

"That Sicilian gardener was a terrible man. I know that. A warped and envious soul. The frankness and pride of that tiny God of Procreation filled him with anger. He could not face its demon and lascivious mouth! Or perhaps it was the artistry—the delight of a golden land in a golden age—that caused him to feel the dross within himself. Whatever it was I shall never know, but as I watched him, stooping slightly because of his club foot, he shattered it with his spade and shovelled its baby, red limbs into the bushes. His face, when he turned to go home, was darker than the cypress-trees in the garden."

Jackson shifted in his chair.

"Maxwell is another such. I do not understand him, and I am afraid of him. I am very glad I never met him. In his desk was a great sheaf of papers—mainly letters to and from victims. And accounts. Somewhere at his house—in a safe, I imagine—there must be hundreds of 'bits of evidence'. All letters were the same letter: men and women terrified the rest of their lives for one indiscretion—often, as in the case of Cunningham, for something comparatively innocent; or even, as with Paxton, for a positive kindness.

As I turned them over I had the sense again of joy crushed out, of light extinguished; only not with a spade—not so suddenly, or so angrily. No: carefully pressed out over the months, not even for the pleasure of pressing. And, because Maxwell was a far more evil man than my gardener, there was destruction, but no death: poison took its place. The delicate fragments of pagan jubilation lay under my laurel bushes: nothing remained. But the faces of these victims are still here, down there at 'The Charter', hatched and notched, and splintered by the bitterness of unending years. And now we four must make our reports, and use our brains, and catch his murderer."

"I know you," said Rambler slowly, fingering his jowl. "You've spoken to me this way before. Twice, to be exact."

"And did I catch the murderer?"

"Yes. Almost immediately afterwards."

Jackson started.

"Oh, don't worry, Inspector." Verity laughed, passing round the wine again. "We're a long way off that yet. And I have no right to be indulging in the luxury of a suspended judgment when there's still work to be done."

"Very well," said Rambler. "Let's get down to it."

"You heard the main details over supper," said Verity, lighting a cigar. "Pelham, have you anything more to add?"

"Yes." The doctor's bird-like face looked out suddenly from the hinterland of shadow. "Examination shows that of the two bullets found in the deceased, both fired from a .45 revolver, one penetrated the left ventricle of the heart to cause death. It must have been instantaneous. He had also quite a nasty bruise on his face too—something he struck when he fell, I hazard."

"Thank you, Doctor," said Rambler. "I'm afraid as evidence it spoils any theories we might have dreamed up that Maxwell did the locking himself—even if we could think of a reason why he should want to do such a thing."

"I'm afraid it does. I am sure he died instantaneously."

"Yes." He turned to Jackson. "Let me run over your list of suspects again. There are Messrs Paxton and Cunningham, Miss Burton, and Miss What's-her-name?"

"Framer, sir. Yes, and someone called Winnidge, apparently a friend of Miss Burton."

"A local man?"

"I should say so, sir."

"Good. Now, Verity's told me most of what has happened to date. I think if he now went over it, it might simplify matters."

"Excellent proposal!" Verity's eyes gleamed with anticipation: the horror of the Sicilian gardener was evidently banished from his mind. "It's all quite simple really: but quite insoluble at the moment. Mr Paxton enters the bedroom by the window and leaves by the door. Mr Cunningham enters by the door and leaves by the window. Yet both door and window are locked. The key of the door is found inside on the floor."

"Obviously this is dependent on one or other of them having a pass-key," said Rambler. "If Paxton had it, he could have locked the window when he came in, and the door on the outside when he left."

"Exactly," said Verity admiringly. "Exactly so."

"If Cunningham had it, he could have used it for entering by the door, and locking it when he left, leaving by the window next door. You say yourself the constable is undecided which window he left from."

"Right again."

"Incidentally, it's very interesting that the man cannot be sure."

"That's the Amnestie police," said Jackson carefully.

"Yes, of course. I heard from Verity that the Carrington men are a very different bunch. By the way, does Paxton admit to locking the window?"

"No, he does not."

"And does Cunningham admit to leaving by Paxton's window?"

"No, he does not."

"Then the one who is lying is pretty wide-awake."

"That's the trouble," said Verity slowly. "I'm not so sure either is telling lies."

"What's that?"

"You see, I happen to know that Cunningham was searched by the constable who caught him at the bottom of the drainpipe. And I happened to see that Paxton was searched in the vestibule when I relieved him of his unfired gun. And neither of them had the key on them."

"Paxton could have got rid of it before shouting for help."

Verity shook his head.

"I taxed him with that when he was in a complete state of nerves after finding the body. He denied it vehemently: and I am rather inclined to give credence to denials made under those circumstances. Besides, he has been under constant surveillance since he reported the murder. If he had concealed it, he could never have reclaimed it."

"That's true."

"Cunningham claims that it was planted on him by Paxton. That was impossible. But that it was planted by someone, I'm prepared to believe."

"Any ideas?"

"What about Miss Framer, the Manageress?" put in the doctor. "She's the person most likely to have it, and I think you said she was involved somehow."

"Good for you, Doctor," Verity shouted. "Have some more wine!... Yes, I believe she is involved. There was that talk about she and Paxton whispering together. And then there's a Memo to see a 'Miss F.' here, among Maxwell's papers. And I recall that she most emphatically described the meeting between Paxton and Maxwell as 'cordial', which it could not possibly have been. The planting of the key on Cunningham, taken together with the deliberate lie, seems to lead to one clear conclusion."

"Which is?"

"That she is covering up for Paxton."

"But why?"

"How am I to know? Unless—"

"Unless?"

The phone rang. It was for Jackson.

"Yes, Matthews?"

There was a pause. Then:

"Are you sure?... I see."

Verity called from the table: "Ask him if anyone can remember if Miss Framer went into the dining-room this morning, when Paxton and Cunningham were there!"

Jackson asked the question. There was a pause, then the Inspector was heard saying:

"Good… good! Let me know when you've got anything else."

He rang off and returned to the table.

"Yes, Locksley says Miss Framer went into the dining-room to put some cutlery on the sideboard. He doesn't seem to have paid much attention to what she did exactly."

"When was this?"

"When we were seeing Paxton in the lounge."

"Excellent! She had ample opportunity to do her planting."

"Yes," said Jackson. "And the evidence I've just received seems to back up your theory."

"What was that?"

"There were nobody else's prints on the pass-key. Only Miss Framer's."

"Are they sure?"

"They're certain."

"Wonderful! Anything else?"

"Yes, they're working on the revolver now. Oh, and the constable who caught Cunningham definitely identifies the window as Maxwell's."

"What makes him so certain?" asked Verity, smiling slightly, and taking a fistful of raisins from the table. "Anyway, I'm not sure it matters much now. There was no need for Cunningham to lie in his statement to us. We know now he didn't have a pass-key with him—so he could gain no advantage from saying he left by Paxton's window."

"True," said Rambler again. "It's all very interesting."

"Isn't it though, Porpoise?" said Verity excitedly. "Here you have a mystery of the century! Listen. A murder is committed in a room. Two men are immediate suspects. Suspect A enters by the window and leaves by the door. Suspect B enters by the door and leaves by the window. Suspect A can lock the window but not the door. Suspect B can lock the door but not the window. Neither can lock both—yet both are locked: and from the inside. And all the while a body, which medical evidence proves could not have done the locking itself before it expired, leaks blood over the carpet of an empty room."

"Empty except for the girl," said the doctor.

"Except for the girl. And she was in a faint."

"Says she was," said the doctor. "There's no way of telling!"

"This is Miss Burton?" asked Rambler.

"Yes. She complicates matters beautifully."

"You mean she makes them easier, Doctor," said Rambler. "Because she does, you know. The problem of who locked the door *and* the window would be quite insoluble without her. But now there's something to get one's teeth into—even if it's only a fantastic story of a man in a mask."

"I should say *because* of the fantastic story," retorted the doctor, not to be outdone. "I see there are times when obvious untruth is the policeman's salvation."

"Certainly," agreed Verity, "if it *is* untruth."

"Surely you don't believe that story she told?"

"We can't afford to doubt it," the old man replied. "We can't afford to doubt anything. Here—I'm neglecting my duty! Have a cigar, won't you?"

He passed round the box. Four flames leapt in the dark.

"Let's look at this thing logically," said Rambler, puffing out. "If we can't afford to exclude Miss Burton's story, we certainly can't afford to exclude Miss Burton herself. She fits in here somewhere."

"Yes, sir," said Jackson. "As you say, she's part of the only possible solution to this mystery of the locked room."

"Exactly. Even granting that Paxton and Cunningham did the murder, neither could have done it without help. Which leads us directly to Miss Burton. This girl was obviously either an accomplice or she did it alone. Personally I think she was an accomplice."

"Why?" asked the doctor.

"Well, from what you say, she does not seem the sort of girl to kill a man and then tie herself up in his cupboard. Of course, that is only a supposition. We'll consider that possibility later. First let's take the first of my alternatives—that she was an accomplice. If so, who was her partner? Paxton? I hardly think so. I cannot imagine why he should call the police so immediately. In doing so, he cancelled out any object he may have had in getting his accomplice to lock the door behind him."

"Good," said Verity, from the other end.

"That leaves us with Cunningham as accomplice. Now, this is more likely. He has to use Miss Burton to gain admittance to the room in the first place. The waitress to whom, on her own confession, Maxwell always gave his orders, could rely on having the door unlocked for her."

"Yes!" Dr Pelham nodded vigorously.

"Now imagine what follows. Supposing she goes into the room at approximately 7.35. Cunningham joins her at about 7.40. He shoots his victim dead after a struggle, and is about to leave when he sees Paxton out on the balcony, preparing to come in through the window. They both hide—one behind the cupboard; the other perhaps behind the bed. Paxton comes in, takes a swift look at Maxwell, realises he is dead, and rushes off to call the police. Obviously they have to work quickly. They daren't be seen coming out of Maxwell's room! So he locks the door with the ordinary key which, I imagine, Maxwell always kept on the inside, then throws it down on the floor, where you found it. He then goes to the window, and climbs out—telling Miss Burton to follow him as soon as he is down safely. Down he goes: and falls neatly into the arms of a policeman. Petrified, Miss Burton sees this from the bedroom. What is she to do? She can't leave by the door. You, Verity, were probably outside it with Paxton——"

"Who was making the dickens of a noise on it."

"Precisely. And she can't leave by the window because of the policeman. And then she hits on a brilliant idea—an idea born of absolute panic: the story of the masked man. In an unreasoning flap she locks the window, gets into the cupboard, ties herself up roughly with a bit of cord and, having first taken the precaution of putting the key on the inside in case she may need it, slams the door on herself. It has, I think you said, an automatic lock."

Verity's blue eyes glittered with pleasure.

"Bravo!" he said. "Brilliant!"

The doctor murmured approval *sotto voce*, and even Jackson was impressed.

Verity stood up and opened a door at his end of the room. A breeze came in from the garden, blowing out the rest of the candles. Only the outlines of statues were visible in the glow of the cigars. The doctor joined him.

"It's funny," Pelham said, looking down the hill towards the dark sea. "As human beings you are all of you conscious of your faults, your liability to error. But as detectives you become incapable, somehow, of seeing other people as men and women very like yourselves. You deal with the facts before you as if they were the faint clues of a perfect crime, the tiny, inerasable vestiges of a plan which has worked superbly. Yet once you see them for what they really are—pointers to the *imperfections* of a crime—everything becomes clarity itself."

"True, true, Doctor," sighed Verity. "We are incurably stupid. Now that Rambler has so ably pointed it out, the Man-in-the-Mask story appears as exactly what it is: the fabrication of a minute. Looked at sympathetically, the facts before us yield something not so very diabolically clever, after all: merely a girl, confused by the work of a moment, not knowing which way to turn to save herself and her accomplice, locking windows which should be left open, leaving guns lying which should be removed. It's a pathetic picture of ineptitude, really. And afterwards—think of afterwards: the girl lying trembling in the blackness of the wardrobe, dreaming up details for her impossible bandit with the mask over his face! And all the time, by her one oversight of locking the window, she had destroyed any chance she had of convincing us of his existence!"

"It will be necessary," said Jackson, "to establish some sort of liaison between Cunningham and the girl. At present we haven't even any proof that they know each other."

"You may depend on it," said Rambler grimly. "They know each other!"

From the dark hall the telephone rang. Jackson rose and groped his way to answer it. There was a pause: he grunted, then replaced the receiver.

"They've examined Cunningham's gun," he said. He turned to Rambler. "That's the one we found in the room, sir."

"Well? They found Cunningham's prints, of course?"

"Yes. And Miss Burton's too."

Verity stepped back into the darkened room and grasped Rambler warmly by the arm.

"Did you hear that, Porpoise?" he said admiringly. "And Miss Burton's too!"

"And Mr Paxton's as well, I'm afraid," said Inspector Jackson.

CHAPTER VI

"I T'S ONLY NATURAL THAT THINGS SHOULD BE AS COM-
plicated as this," Verity was saying. It was the following
morning, and he and Rambler were descending the hill to the
town. "After all, the whole atmosphere is as difficult as it could be."

"It certainly is," said Rambler, looking out to sea. "What are
the chances of a little bathing sometime today? Don't forget
I'm still on my holiday."

"All right," said Verity. "But I regret I have only one costume. I'll bathe first, while you're seeing Jackson. Then you
can go. Ah!... Look over there! That white building at the end
of the road nearest to us!"

"'The Charter'?"

"Yes, 'The Charter' of Amnestie: a small, undistinguished
English hotel. Why should anyone want to come down here?
Yet Maxwell chose it. I wonder why?... Because Miss Burton
was here—"

"Or Miss Framer was here—"

"Or both."

"And Paxton chose it."

"Probably because Maxwell was here."

"And Cunningham, for the same reason. Maxwell probably
wrote them pleasant letters from here."

"And then there's this man Winnidge. Does anyone know who he is?"

"He's a local. We'll know by tonight."

"Good."

"And there's somebody else you can't afford to miss."

"Oh, who's that?"

"King Richard the Fourth of England."

At the hotel Inspector Jackson was already hard at work in the lounge, interviewing the other residents. Verity went quietly off for his bathe, and for the next half-hour Rambler looked on as three bewildered widows, living precariously on fixed incomes, and a fierce Colonel Rainchart, with a balding head and a ramrod spine, revealed that they knew nothing of what was going on, and were not greatly interested. The Colonel, it is true, did think he had heard a shot two nights before—but it had turned out to be "only the dog—dashed nuisance!"

None of the servants knew anything either. Mr Maxwell had had all his meals in his room, and Miss Burton was the only one allowed to wait on him.

Something of interest was, however, elicited from a Mr Swabber, a retired builder, now taking an extended holiday by the sea. Mr Swabber occupied the room next to Mr Maxwell, on the farthest side from the main staircase, and, now they came to mention it, he had heard a noise yesterday morning in his neighbour's room.

"What time was this?" asked Jackson.

"Oh, it must have been about six in the morning," said Swabber, sticking his thumbs in his waistcoat pocket and preparing to enjoy a brief moment of importance. "Yes, about six—or six-thirty. No later. No, sir, no later than six-thirty."

"What was this noise you heard?"

"Well, first it was the door of his room opening. I didn't much mind that, really, because it happened all the time, you might say."

"All the time?"

"Yes. Maxwell was always coming in in the early mornings. He'd often stay out half the night. It was when he took his exercise, so Miss Framer said."

"I see."

"Yes, but yesterday morning was different."

"Oh? How—different?"

"Well, there was another person in with him. I could swear to it! The walls are pretty thin, you know, and me lying awake next door, I heard 'em walking about."

"How many of them were there?"

"Oh, just two. Him and another man, I should say."

"A man?"

"Yes, I heard one of 'em talking. He kept his voice down, but I'm sure it was a man... And then there was noises."

"What noises?"

Mr Swabber leant forward and winked heavily.

"The noises was the trouble... Moans and groans—and then the other man talking low. And then a noise like someone staggering about a bit, as if they was a bit pickled. Then all of a sudden—a bang, like someone falling down. And then the moaning stopped."

"And then?"

"The door opened and one of them went out."

"Is that all?"

"A long time later, I heard a car drive off. Mind you, it wasn't outside the hotel. No, sir; farther off it was!"

"It had been parked farther down the street, you mean?"

"That's right. Farther down…"

"How long after was this?"

"Oh, a good long time… Must have been fifteen minutes."

"I see. Anything else?"

"No, not that I can bring to mind. I fell asleep shortly after."

"Excellent," said Rambler, when Swabber had gone. "That opens up several new avenues."

Jackson nodded, satisfied with himself.

"Oh dear," said Verity, from the garden, "haven't we enough already?"

"Hullo? How's the water?"

"Much too warm!"

He came through the French window wringing the water from his beard. He had changed back into his baggy flannels, and through the window they could see where his immense mauve costume hung sodden from a straining branch of the apple-tree.

They told him Mr Swabber's story.

"New avenues indeed!" said Verity excitedly. "There is much that may be deduced from this tale of groaning in a neighbouring room. Remember, the doctor said that there were two gun-wounds: but only one of them was fatal. Up to now we have been assuming that the two bullets were fired from the same gun. But what if one of them were fired earlier, and by another gun—say about six-thirty by the man with the car?"

"That would account for all the blood in the room," said Jackson.

"And at the foot of the stairs," said Verity. "He was probably carried up."

"It certainly fits," agreed Rambler. "It looks as if we have another suspect on our hands."

"Might I suggest Winnidge?"

"You might indeed."

"Oh, by the way, I forgot to tell you," said Verity, lighting the first cigar of the day. "I asked Sergeant Matthews to search Miss Burton's room before letting her go back to it."

"You asked Matthews?" Jackson was clearly shocked.

"Yes. I told him I'd take the blame myself, so don't say anything to him. It was worth it. He found a note in one of the drawers: a note from Maxwell."

"No!" Rambler was all attention. "What does it say?"

"Oh, nothing very much. It just warns her 'for her own good' not to make any objections to waiting on him. He also says that if she tried running away again—note the 'again'—it would be the worse for her. He wouldn't hesitate to make use of what he knew."

"So that's why he came down!" said Rambler. "Obviously she was hiding out here, and Maxwell got to know of it!"

"Well, anyway, she didn't take his advice," Jackson put in. "That threatening letter we found from Winnidge seems to prove that she told *him* at any rate."

"Things are beginning to centre more and more on Winnidge," said Rambler, pulling thoughtfully at his jowl. "We must see him at the earliest possible moment."

"Always assuming that's his right name," said Verity. "In the meantime, let's have your two accomplices in. They should make interesting listening."

"Good. We'll see Cunningham first. Then, I suppose, the oft-tried confronting scene."

Jackson nodded and sent Constable Locksley for Cunningham. When, in a moment, he appeared and sat down on the wicker-settee opposite Jackson and Rambler, he was obviously more composed than on the preceding day. It seemed to Verity, sitting in the corner, that his eyes were more controlled and that his moustache had been brushed, along with the rather sparse, sandy hair on his head.

"This is Detective Inspector Rambler," said Jackson. "Mr Cunningham."

Rambler smiled. His leading suspect looked at him with dislike.

"Now, all he wants is the answers to a few questions—"

"Well, he won't get them!" said Cunningham. "You heard all I have to say yesterday. You can tell him that! I'll be blowed if I repeat it all for his benefit!"

Mr Verity watched the fury in the man's grey eyes: an easy man to bluff, if need be.

Rambler leant forward over the table, hunching his massive shoulders as he did so, and the voice that issued from his tiny mouth became smoother than ever.

"Mr Cunningham," he breathed, closing soft hands together, "we are investigating a murder. You are one of a number of people suspected of doing that murder. I really think you had better tell me what I want to know."

"I can see why you've been brought in," said Cunningham, looking at him sharply. "They're finding it too much for them!"

Rambler ignored this. "I want you to amplify one of your statements, if you don't mind." (In procedure of this sort both he and Verity were as one: 'two soft-tonged Magi' as someone in Chelsea had once said of them, 'whom Circe had turned into bison.') "You told Mr Verity yesterday that you were once working for a firm of brokers. Is this true?"

"Why shouldn't it be?" asked Cunningham sullenly.

Where was this firm?

"Somewhere in the City."

"You are very co-operative," said Rambler dangerously. "Why did they fire you, Mr Cunningham?"

"I see no need to answer that… Why I was fired concerns me alone."

"For the moment, yes. It may, however, concern a jury later on."

"What do you mean by that?"

"Oh, come, Mr Cunningham, do be reasonable! You were fired from your firm because you were taking dope in such large quantities that you were becoming unreliable. So much is anyone's easy guess. Why you took the stuff in the first place is, I concede, your business alone—at any rate for the present. But where you got it from is an entirely different matter."

"Got it from?"

"Yes, Cunningham, where? The knowledge that you took dope—as Mr Verity has already observed to you—would really be pretty poor security to a blackmailer. Anyone can see it for himself. Further, I doubt very much if you have the self-respect left to mind if anyone can see it or not: and you certainly wouldn't pay a blackmailer to prevent him revealing such a thing."

"My observations to Mr Cunningham," said Verity from behind the pages of his 'Sphere', "were made with the sole purpose of telling him, as politely as possible, that I knew he was lying."

"And what," asked Rambler of his friend, "was the point of being polite?"

"Because I did not see the necessity of proving his real motive. Everyone who knew Maxwell had a motive for kill-ing him. It was sufficient to know that Mr Cunningham was involved: I guessed the rest."

"And what did you guess?"

There was a pause. Jackson stopped taking notes. Cunningham looked agonised.

"Even if a dope-addict does not mind people knowing he takes it," said Verity carefully, "he certainly does mind people knowing how he gets it."

"As Mr Cunningham has just demonstrated," said Rambler.

"Quite so. It occurred to me that Mr Maxwell himself was supplying the stuff, but I rejected the idea. Trafficking would have been far too energetic an occupation for him."

"And far too wholesome," said Rambler.

"I also recollected that among his papers we found a fairly standard demand-note addressed to Mr Cunningham. Now a man who supplies a hopeless addict does not have to solicit him for business by using threats of exposure."

"In other words," Rambler inquired, "Maxwell was not asking the price for his continued supply, but for his continued secrecy?"

"Yes, in other words."

"And can you imagine what it is he had to be secret about?"

"I should say it was the knowledge you yourself were seeking but a moment back. That is: who was supplying Mr Cunningham with his dope? To know that, and to be able to prove it, would be enough to put Mr Cunningham in one's power."

"Rest assured," said Mr Rambler to Mr Verity. "We have Mr Cunningham in our power without any such knowledge."

He turned to his victim—who was beginning to tremble uncontrollably—and resumed the examination. Jackson sat aghast at his table, and endeavoured to take notes.

"So: the person who was supplying you was also 'known' to Maxwell. As for his identity—well, it could be anyone! Mr Verity's guess is as good as mine. The name might appear in his papers, of course, but that's a long shot. Tell me, Mr Cunningham: how long have you known Miss Burton?"

"Miss Burton?... I don't understand. I don't know any Miss Burton!"

"You know," said Rambler quietly, "contrary to general belief, detectives find this kind of stalling very tedious. Now supposing, for a change, we had the whole story in one piece."

"Story?" shouted Cunningham. "I tell you I don't know any Miss Burton!… To hell with your questions… You think you're clever—doing that double act with your bearded friend in the corner!… Well, so you are—damn clever! Go ahead, both of you! You don't need any help from me! You're fine by yourselves!"

"Bring in Miss Burton, please," Rambler said to Locksley.

They all sat in silence—broken only by Cunningham's muttered "Go ahead… You're fine!"—until she appeared. Rambler was evidently keyed up to 'manage' a scene; Verity put down the 'Sphere'.

On entering she cast one look at Cunningham, but showed no detectable trace of emotion. Indeed, in her waitress' uniform, she looked the very image of self-possession: she stood a little to Jackson's left, her head thrown back almost defiantly, and her braided hair catching the sunlight from the garden. Some colour had now returned to her cheeks, and her lively blue eyes were sparkling.

The two old men looked at her admiringly.

("If he's going to accuse her of peddling dope," said Verity to himself, "he'll be making a very big mistake. Unlike him, I trust my memories. And I remember the Matron of Syracuse as well as I do the Sicilian gardener. She may be a murderess, but she *didn't* peddle dope. You can't be righteous about peddling dope.")

"Good-morning," said Rambler, affectionately. "How are you this morning?"

"Much better, thank you." She smiled.

"That's fine. Now I want you to run over your statement about what happened yesterday morning, if you would be so good."

"Now?"

He nodded winningly.

("I shan't interfere, though," Verity continued his soliloquy. "Even if he accuses her of supplying Cunningham with his beastly stuff, I shan't interfere. It sometimes helps to have one's suspects thinking one is barking up the wrong tree... Absurd expression—'barking up the wrong tree'! What on earth can be the use of barking up a right tree?...")

While Mr Verity was turning over these thoughts, the girl was going over her story of the day before. Rambler treated her gently enough, but his eyes never left her face. She told him all there was to tell: of the summons by Maxwell, the entry of the masked man, the quarrel, the shooting, the faint, the awakening in the wardrobe—everything was included, and without so much as a blush. Even Rambler had to admit she made a good liar:—a wonderful liar, considering that her accomplice was sitting behind her on the settee. When she had finished, he thanked her politely.

"Your account is very clear, Miss Burton. An unfortunate business. Did you happen to notice what kind of gun the man was holding when he threatened Mr Maxwell?"

"No. I'm afraid I didn't."

"A pity. Did you know Mr Maxwell?"

"Well, not very well, sir... I used to serve him his meals, of course."

("She may be lying," said Verity to himself. "But is it possible—is it just possible—that Winnidge's letter refers to another Alice?... I wonder...")

"Why 'of course'?" asked Rambler. "I gather no one else was allowed in the room."

"I—I'm afraid I can't explain that, sir..."

"You have no idea?"

"None at all, sir."

"Well, I have!" shouted Cunningham, getting up furiously and turning to Verity. "I told you I saw her go into his room two nights ago. I told you I saw that!"

"So you did," said Verity equably.

"I heard them quarrelling, I tell you. They were at it hammer and tongs, almost as soon as she entered the room!"

"Ohh!..." Alice screamed aloud. "Ohh!... My God!..." She backed hastily round behind the lounge-table. "I'd know that voice anywhere!"

"What voice?"

"Don't let him near me! He knows I'm speaking the truth!"

"Truth!" shouted Cunningham. "It's me who's telling the truth! I heard her with Maxwell! I *saw* her go in!"

"Don't listen to him! He's lying—anyone can see he's lying!"

"*I'm* lying! That's fine! That's magnificent, coming—"

"Silence!" roared Rambler, banging the table. It fell at once. "Now, whose voice do you recognise, Miss Burton? This is Mr Cunningham, a guest at the hotel."

"Yes," said Alice shakily. "I've seen him before. But I've never served him. And I never heard his voice till yesterday morning."

"In the bedroom?"

"Yes. As I stand here—that's the man in the mask!"

There was another silence for a moment, and then Cunningham started to laugh.

"My dear Inspector!" he said, his moustache quivering as he gulped down his merriment in little bursts, "my dear Inspector... First you ask me whether I associate with waitresses and then... then you actually bring one in to tell me... that I... put on a mask and tied her up in a cupboard!... Brilliant, Inspector! My congratulations, Inspector! Brilliant!... Priceless!..."

Verity noted that the laughter was shrill and hysterical. But Rambler was incapable of any such attention: he was just staring in silence at Miss Burton, who was repeating over and over again: "That's him! That's the man I heard!"

The noise went on for several minutes. Then, at last, Jackson snapped to Locksley "Get them out of here—both of them!" and the babble subsided. Mr Verity watched them being taken away with a look of very genuine surprise.

"And where are your accomplices now?" asked a voice from the garden.

CHAPTER VII

IT WAS RICHARD TUDOR, DRESSED IN A LONG GREEN BATH-robe, returning from the sea. Mr Verity performed the introduction, but Rambler was too stunned to pay much attention.

"You must pardon me," said Tudor. "I couldn't help over-hearing you earlier on as I passed through the garden. You were talking about confronting your suspects, as I remember. Of course it's none of my business, but it does seem to me to be rather a question of class."

"You mean that a City man doesn't conspire with a waitress?"

"No, the other way about. A gentlewoman may, for rea-sons best known to herself, prefer to live incognito, but she does not for that reason ally herself with persons of Mr Cunningham's stamp."

"That is very perceptive of you," said Verity. "However, Miss Burton is not a gentlewoman, as you suggest: merely fair to middling, I fancy."

Rambler recovered from his stupor.

"I am pleased to meet you," he said.

"You have my sympathy," said Tudor. "You were obviously working on the right lines."

"I was?"

"But certainly. You can never afford to neglect the terrible fact that England today is full of conspirators. *Full*," he repeated.

"I shan't," said Rambler solemnly. "And now, if you will excuse me, I am going for a bathe. It may help…"

He went out quickly through the French window, snatching Verity's costume from the apple-tree as he did so. ("A shame," thought Verity. "In other circumstances he would have been more appreciative.") Aloud, he too excused himself, but with more ceremony.

"You are a gentleman, sir," said Richard Tudor, tossing back his locks from his pallid face. "You have been trained in the proper tradition."

Mr Verity, who was not sensible of having been trained at all, bowed slightly.

"Who were your parents?" pursued Tudor.

"I never knew my father," said Verity, moving to the door. "It is said he died of laughing on his sixth reading of the 'Bab Ballads'."

"I meant—what family were your parents?"

"Oh, I see. Well, my father was nothing. His family were all Stock Exchange. My mother was different. When I was ten she fell violently in love with a carpenter."

"A carpenter?"

"Yes. The neighbours put it down to religious mania. He was one of the men working on the annexe to our house. I recall that the extension acquired eleven windows more than it needed before she let him go. Seven bay and four dormer."

Mr Tudor stared in bewilderment.

"Come," said Verity kindly, "be so good as to accompany me to the Post Office. I have some business to conduct with a friend abroad."

"Political business?" asked Tudor in a hushed voice.

"No, lapidary. I am in process of buying a statue."

Tudor looked crestfallen, but consented to accompany the old man into the open air.

The High Street of Amnestie was about three hundred yards of narrow, cobbled road, descending in a steep slope from 'The Charter' to the square. It was flanked on either side by tumble-down shops, above which showed the close-netted windows of the rooms where their owners lived. The post office was at the very bottom in the square itself, and the two men strode swiftly down the hill towards it.

"This afternoon you can examine my documents," said Tudor magnanimously.

"That is very good of you. Unfortunately, this afternoon I shall be rather busy."

"With the investigation of this man's death?"

"Yes."

"A triviality not worth the enquiry. He was an evil little person. You should not waste your talents on such an affair."

"As I remember it," said Verity with a smile, "we are all of us 'sub lege'—even the King."

"I have never subscribed to that," Tudor replied grandly. "This notion of everybody's being under the same law is fine enough in theory; but in practice it is merely an obstacle to efficiency. An important country can only be ruled by a strong central government having unlimited power."

"So your ancestors believed," said Verity.

"Yes, and the fewer wielding the power the better."

"They believed that, too. I suppose the Tudor sovereigns were the most powerful England ever had."

"And the most efficient."

"Yes. Of course, they never made the mistake of saying they were above the Law. They just made the Law and said they were under it."

He plunged into the post office, followed by Tudor.

Amnestie post office was a very small general store: it smelt of groceries and, because it was so dark, an electric lamp burned always over the counter. Mr Verity squeezed himself with difficulty among the open baskets of lentils and split peas, and approached the end of the counter that had a brass grille before it.

"Good morning!" he boomed into the darkness. "Is anyone here?"

There was a faint noise on the other side of the counter, and he made out two round eyes, gleaming at him through a pair of steel-framed spectacles. Mr Verity took out his eye-glass.

"I wish to send a telegram."

"Aye!" The voice was shrill, but male.

"Yes. To Smyrna."

A form was thrust through the grille: it was for Home use, and had to be returned. This flustered the little man behind the counter, who had "thought it was in Yorkshire."

Finally Mr Verity did his best, in the gloom, to write out his message to Professor Mantys. ("Besides being virtually the only man on Syrian stuff actually resident there," he explained in an aside to Tudor, "his methods of collecting it are entirely unscrupulous. So much so that his friends call him 'Preying Mantys'.")

In the meanwhile there was much rummaging through lists and comparison of prices behind the grille, and endless quotation of rates per twenty-five words. Mr Verity received the impression that it was all done in a desperate effort to get him out of the shop. If this was the intention, it finally succeeded. The little man began reading the message through, but there came a gasp at the second line, and feeble noises of protest. He had stuck at the word "Hierapolis".

"Begging your pardon," he said, peering out of the darkness, "but is this English?"

"In spelling," Verity assured him.

"Aye, well, you'd better write it plainer. I've got to spell it out, y'know, and the girl at Carrington's rather deaf!"

Mr Verity was now convinced that the message would never get there at all: so he asked for it back again, very politely, and bought a tin of fruit salts instead.

"That's easier, isn't it?" said the little man affably.

"Certainly," Mr Verity agreed. "Have you ever heard of a man called Winnidge hereabouts?"

The man scratched his head: "Winnidge?... No, can't say I have. Oh, but wait a bit... Yes, I've heard the name once or twice. Can't say where... Does he live here?"

"I believe so," said Verity.

"Well, I don't go out much, y'know. I could ask my son."

"Thank you, but don't give yourself the trouble." Mr Verity delved into his pocket. "I owe you half a crown, I believe."

All this time Tudor had been waiting in the doorway, forming a silhouette of proud isolation against the noonday sky.

"There you are!" he said contemptuously when Verity rejoined him in the street. "The reign of democracy! What could be sillier than giving common people public positions involving tasks which are obviously too difficult for them?"

"That man is fully adequate for his normal duties," Verity replied, as they began their slow toil up the hill. "It was I, not the Government, who gave him the task which was too much for him."

"Locals!" Tudor snorted indignantly.

"In your admiration for a centralised government, do not forget that Elizabethan England was virtually run by J.P.s."

"Under close supervision."

"I wonder exactly how close any supervision could have been with roads like theirs."

Tudor shrugged and said nothing. He was clearly not used to being crossed. Verity warmed to his subject.

"In any case, you don't seem to appreciate that a shift of authority has occurred over the centuries. Granting that you are of royal absolutist stock, and even that you are rightful king of this country, I can imagine no worse ruler for the twentieth century—if you don't mind my saying so—than a Tudor. As for a combination of Tudor and Spaniard—that is quite unthinkable! The union of Mary with Philip was bad enough!"

"Mary was a much-misunderstood woman," Tudor said shortly.

"That is irrelevant. If she was misunderstood then, she would be misunderstood today. So would you."

"I fail to understand."

"Because *I* am the real ruler of this country—I and the hundreds like me who exercise sway in the name of the people. It is this authority—from which we derive our just powers—that makes our individual weaknesses irrelevant. You are a Catholic: you know that the character of an ordained priest doesn't matter. Well, nor does that of an enrolled policeman."

"I think that is more than a little blasphemous!" Tudor said stiffly.

Verity ignored the remark.

"I myself am not an enrolled policeman: by my celebrated alliances with the Force I have, however, participated in its merit. The result is that, temporarily at any rate, my power is unlimited. Think of it! At this moment I could issue an order and have all the women in 'The Charter' Hotel standing on one leg in the garden, simply by declaring it necessary. They would do it like a shot—because they have really commended themselves to me for protection just as the barons did to you in days gone by. Standing like that at my order would be their form of boon-work. They do it because they know the alternative. If they don't obey me I shall leave them to the mercy of each other here in Amnestie, or anywhere else it happens to be—and that might mean their being shot as Maxwell was shot."

"I think you are utterly heartless. I have no desire to listen to any more of this talk!"

"I am sorry you find it offensive. It is nevertheless true—almost drearily obvious. There would be absolutely no point in acclaiming a Tudor now: the type of protection he could offer is no longer needed. Scotland Yard has supplanted the Star Chamber—the old reservation still remaining."

"And that is?"

"Well, I can command the women of Amnestie to behave like storks for an unrevealed reason because they trust the wisdom of my intentions. But if I were to suggest that they did the same thing in the garden stark naked, they would understand my intentions only too well and promptly refuse. Such things do not appertain to the mystery of Kingship."

They were now at the Hotel. Mr Verity handed over his tin of fruit salts and, with a courteous "Good day", passed inside.

Mr Tudor stood dumbfounded at the threshold, choking with rage to which he was evidently incapable of giving vent. When finally he did bring something out, it was neither opposing argument nor imprecation.

"Very well!" he said quietly, to himself. "Very well! I know something that can help you—help you very much. Just you see if I tell it!"

But Mr Verity was out of earshot.

As the old man passed through into the hall, Miss Burton came down the stairs, still flushed from her recent interview. He approached her smiling.

"If you could spare me a few minutes, I should be very grateful, Miss Burton."

"Well, sir…" She looked startled. "It's getting on for lunchtime and the tables aren't laid yet."

"I'm sure Miss Framer will excuse you for a moment. This is really very important."

He took her arm and led her back through the lounge and into the garden. Inspector Jackson was still at his table: he stared with surprised, but preoccupied eyes, as they passed through.

It was warm and bright in the garden, and the strong smell of wild-mint filled the air. At the bottom, near the gate which led to the beach, was a pool: standing by its edge they watched the reflection of thin clouds move slowly across it, like javelins of cotton-wool.

"Beautiful," said Alice. Drooping silver fish were swimming sleepily around in circles. "It's as if they were swimming in the sky through the branches of the trees."

"How much are you going to tell me?" asked Verity.

She faced him coldly.

"Tell you? But I've told you all I know."

"You've told me nothing," he said gently. "Nothing that's important. That's why I brought you down here, away from the atmosphere of policemen and cross-examinations. You see, I must know some more."

She gave him a quick glance.

"The police don't believe me, then?"

"They don't disbelieve you," said Verity.

"But it's a pretty tall story to swallow, all the same?"

"I'm afraid it is. Almost as tall as your being a waitress."

"Does that show through so much?" She looked suddenly tired and dispirited. Then she tossed her head with a touch of anger. "It's no use! Even if you are on my side, I have only your word for it!"

"Look, my dear, it isn't a question of sides. I need the truth. If you persist in acting like a Woman of Mystery—and not a very successful one, either—then you have only yourself to blame for what happens. You obviously have a great deal to do with this business: Inspector Rambler thinks so, and he is rarely wrong."

She looked at him in silence. Her eyes were the softest feature in a rather hard face. Assuredly Miss Burton could be ruthless, if she desired to be.

"Tell me," he said.

"There's little to tell."

"About Maxwell."

Verity waited. All the crickets seemed to stop scraping too. He realised that there was very little time left before Rambler came back from his bathe—when whatever confidence he had managed to inspire would be instantly lost.

"I thought once I could do it," she said. "I thought once I could escape from the past, and begin a new life."

"What was the old? I only press for details which I must have."

"For instance?"

There was a note of challenge in her voice.

"You are right to be suspicious," he said gravely. "I should be, too, were I in your position."

"You speak as if my arrest were a foregone conclusion!"

Verity looked at her regretfully. "It almost is," he said.

If he had expected some sort of expostulation, he was quite mistaken. She looked away from him up the garden, her lips moving slightly and her hands clenched. After a moment he hazarded a question.

"Where were you working when he found you?"

"In the office. I—I had been very foolish."

"Of course, or he wouldn't have been interested in you."

"I know that now." She turned to him again. "But not then. Then he said he only wanted to help me—and I believed him. I did it…"

"Yes?"

"For my father. You see, I was the only support. His wife had died long ago, and he was quite incapable…"

"You stole?"

She nodded, startled at his bluntness.

"Quite a deal of money. When he helped me find a job with a friend of his I was more grateful than I could ever hope to explain. It was a good job—a salary of almost eight pounds a week. I didn't know that his—this 'friend' had been forced to take me by Mr Maxwell. You see, Mr Maxwell knew something about him too, and—"

"There's no need to explain that. I know a great deal about Mr Maxwell."

"Did you know him yourself?" she asked quickly.

"I never met him in life. I never wish to see his picture."

"He was a terrible man. He had—well, no motive for what he did. I used to feel sometimes he was revenging himself on all of us for something that happened long ago."

"Did you know him—very well?"

His emphasis made her pause once more. A dragon-fly shot quivering across the surface of the pool. Then she nodded again.

"I see. For how long?"

"Months. Until I met Ted."

"Ted?"

"Ted Winnidge. He was the most wonderful person I had ever met. The kindest, oh! the kindest——"

"Did he know about Maxwell?"

"No. I didn't dare to tell him."

"That was foolish."

"I know it now. But then—then *he* was always there, just waiting. He could do anything he wanted. At any time he could have told the police, don't you see? He threatened to—any time I left him!"

"And wasn't that worth risking?"

"With Ted? Perhaps. But I was frightened—I didn't dare. Not for months I didn't. Of course he couldn't understand it at all—why I kept putting things off… It was terrible…"

Mr Verity squeezed her arm sympathetically.

"But you did tell him in the end?"

"Yes. In the end."

"When was this?"

"When I couldn't stand it any longer. I didn't care what happened to me then. I came down here—"

"Down to Amnestie?"

"Yes. This is where he lives now. I came down here determined to make a clean breast of things—to start again. I went to see Ted. I told him everything. It was horrible, but I did it. I told him everything."

Once again Verity saw that look of triumph and relief on her small, clear face. Once again it made him afraid. "She could commit murder as easily as I throw pebbles into this pond," he reflected. And why not? What woman worth her salt would not, when all this was at stake?

"What did he say?" he asked out loud.

"Of course he was very angry."

"You told him about your own theft?"

"I had to. I wasn't afraid. I'd paid in full."

"And then?"

"He wanted to go to London right away to see Maxwell. If he had, I think he'd have killed him on the spot. In the end I think he only wrote a letter."

"And instead, Maxwell came down to see you?"

"Yes. I promised Ted that I would never see him again. I took a job here, and then I wrote a letter to him saying I was never coming back. I told him he could do what he liked. That's what I told him!"

"And you put the address here on your letter?"

"Yes. On purpose. I wanted him to know where I was. I wanted him to know I was living here, engaged to Ted. I wanted him to know I was free of him."

"Free of him?" Verity's blue eyes looked at her piercingly. "Is that why you brought him his meals every day when he appeared here?"

She flushed.

"I wanted time to think. One word and he would have ruined my name here—and don't you see, this is Ted's home now. This is where he wants to settle—where I want to live."

"So you spent your time 'reasoning with him'?"

Alice looked puzzled at the sarcasm in his tone.

"I mean you talked to him? Cunningham heard you talking with him the night before the murder. It sounded like quite a row," he said.

"That man—he's just a liar!"

"Nevertheless, you did go there?"

"Yes. I went to make a last appeal to him to go away and leave me in peace."

"Did he listen?"

"No. He told me he would never let me go—never!" Her eyes narrowed at the recollection. "I hated him then as I had never hated even him before. I would have killed him then and there if I'd had anything to do it with! I would! I don't care who knows it!"

"But what did you do in fact?"

"I ran out of the house and down to Ted's house. I told him that Maxwell was here again, and bothering me!"

"He didn't know before that?"

"No. I told him all that had happened on those last four days—how he'd made me bring him his meals and then, in his room…"

"And then what happened?"

Alice Burton stood rigid in the garden, her eyes closed and her fists clenched tight.

"I was wild—excited like I've never been before! I wanted him to kill him—yes, to kill him then—that evening—in front of me! He told me to go back to the hotel."

"And then?"

There was a pause. In the heat the insects were buzzing furiously; thin-stalked flowers were drooping; the continual flare of the sky was intolerable. Mr Verity turned his head and saw the white face of Miss Framer glaring down at them from a first floor window.

"And then?" he repeated.

But Miss Burton was calmer now, aware again of her position.

"He told me not to be a fool," she said carefully, "and sent me home."

"Is that the truth?"

"Yes."

"So he and Maxwell never met?"

"No—not then."

"What do you mean by that?"

She caught sight of Miss Framer at the window, and shivered a little.

"I must go in now…"

"Did they ever meet?" Verity asked precisely.

"Yes, but Ted never knew it at the time."

They started walking back to the house under the baleful glare of the Manageress, who did not budge.

"I'm afraid I still don't understand."

"Well, you see, Maxwell always used a false name when he went out at nights. He hired a taxi about three times, to drive him along the front."

"I know that. But Ted?"

"Was the driver. He owns one of the two taxis here."

"I see. But they never knew each other?"

"Oh, Maxwell knew who Ted was; I'm sure of that. That was probably the main reason why he liked going out. I think he enjoyed just sitting in the back of the car while Ted drove him around, not knowing who he was. That was like him."

"And you're sure Ted didn't know?"

"Perfectly. Ted never knew who the man was—not till the Tuesday night, that is."

"Then you told him?"

"Yes."

"I understand," said Verity, moving aside to let her pass indoors. "He never knew until a few hours before the murder."

CHAPTER VIII

SHE TURNED QUICKLY, WITH A SUDDEN REALISATION OF what she had just said.

"No! I didn't mean that! Ted didn't drive Maxwell that night—I swear he didn't!"

Inside the lounge Jackson was still sitting at the table. By his side stood a little clerical gentleman.

"This is the vicar," said Jackson. "It seems he has something to tell us."

"Yes," said the little man, clasping his hands and bobbing like a lady's maid. "I'm sorry I've been so long coming, but you see I've had a bit of a tussle with my conscience."

"Well, you can save it until Inspector Rambler gets here," said Verity. "It's far too hot to repeat things."

His blue eyes sparked malevolence at the vicar. Mr Verity's detestation of the present-day Church was well known; and to her officers—"all of them on the losing side"—he showed nothing but contempt.

The vicar bobbed again: though he really only dipped his head, it looked as if he were using his whole body. "My name is Robertson," he said.

"And this is Mr Verity," said Jackson.

"Oh!"

The little man looked pleased to know him. The monotony of his smile immediately began to irritate the detective.

"Have you had lunch?" he demanded.

"Well, no, as a matter of fact, not."

"Then you'll have it with us." He turned to Alice, who had been waiting behind him. "Be so good as to lay four places in here, Miss Burton. The vicar is staying to lunch." He turned back again to the Rev. Mr Robertson. "I trust three and sixpence is not beyond your means?"

"No, indeed; but the fact is I have a perfectly adequate meal awaiting me at the vicarage."

"Good. You can give your cook the night off. I have been told that you can enjoy here the finest shrimps on this stretch of coast."

The good man looked unhappy.

"Oh dear—I'm afraid I am allergic to shrimps."

"Pooh!" said Verity magnificently. "Allergy is merely one of modern man's substitutes for individuality!"

Fortunately at this moment Rambler came in from the garden.

Over lunch Verity renewed his observations on the decline of ancient authority—but this time to a clerical listener. The Rev. Mr Robertson found himself being examined like a suspect.

"You have a large number of worshippers within your parish?" the old man asked.

"No, alas!" said the vicar, pronouncing the word to rhyme with 'pass', "my flock is a small one."

"Such, I presume, it always has been. But in the days of the Wars of the Roses it was at any rate more devout—and the parson more influential. How would you have liked to have lived then?"

"You forget," said the vicar, greatly daring, "that in those days I should have had to be a Roman Catholic."

"And that thought displeases you?"

"But naturally."

"At any rate, people would have been aware of you—and you yourself would have been aware of them. In those days morals were as low (or high) as they are now: the only difference is that then people settled their important bills with you in the Vestry; now the only sort of payment they recognise as important is with Miss Framer in the vestibule. I really feel sorry for you."

"Sorry for me?" Mr Robertson smiled nervously.

Rambler and Jackson continued to eat in dogged silence.

"Certainly I feel sorry for you. In the old days you were expected to sally out of your pulpit: you weren't imprisoned in it. It was part of your job to grasp the Beast by its horn and send it back to Babylon."

"Really, Mr Verity—"

"Nowadays," said the old man relentlessly, "we are all told that the Englishman's home is his castle—and this is considered sufficient to guarantee for him a privacy that can profit him nothing. In the days when all respectable Englishmen really lived in castles, you never found anyone asserting anything so silly."

Mr Robertson drew himself up with passable dignity.

"I can only assume you are a Catholic yourself," he said.

"You are quite wrong, my dear vicar," said Mr Verity, swallowing the last of his shrimps. He lowered his voice.

"Please don't imagine I am blaming you for your faith, or for the collapse of it in others. They have had more temptations than you."

Mr Robertson looked inexpressibly shocked.

"No—you misunderstand me. It's not the Inner Light I'm concerned with for the moment, but the Outer Darkness. The Inner Light may help—but it's not enough to deal with something like Maxwell."

"I beg your pardon?"

"A moment ago I said that in the Middle Ages you would have been more aware of other people. They would have let you be more aware of them, if you see what I mean."

"No," said the vicar. "I'm afraid I don't."

Inspector Jackson permitted himself a grin.

"Well, you'd have been a fighter, parson—a man of God and a man of the people. You'd have fought their battles for them, not only with the Horned Beast, but with the ghosts that flickered about the gravestones and the witches that rode over the chimneys. You'd have been everywhere and known everybody: you'd have wielded the trident of dogma and the rod of chastisement with equal dexterity. And when they asked you, you would have swamped the whole village in holy water. Something like Maxwell wouldn't have stood a chance. He'd have been stoned out of the parish—or else tied down whilst you made an attempt at exorcism."

"You still believe in the man's unmitigated evil?" said Rambler. "I don't understand it. You never even knew him."

"Thank God, I did not! I am a diabolist, parson: I once looked on the face of the devil. His face was black. Throughout a long life I have collected many statues, but never have I possessed the only statuary I fully understand: I mean the work of the great primitive civilisations that knew some of the truth about evil. The Greeks were foolish enough to confuse it with ignorance; the Romans even identified it with neglect of duty. But the Assyrians who took blunt instruments and hacked out those towering giants in stone—they knew evil. Their giants carry thongs: they grip savage beasts in their huge hands and glare as they tear them apart. The Phoenicians knew evil that put up Moloch, and fried their babies between his legs."

There was a pause. Alice brought the coffee.

"Why do you always get like this at mealtimes?" asked Rambler heavily, as if he really wanted to know the answer. Verity lit a cigar, but otherwise kept an impressive silence. "Now, vicar," his friend resumed, "you said you had something to tell us. I'm afraid that Mr Verity has not allowed you to say very much about it as yet. Could you please enlighten us now?"

But Mr Robertson was too bewildered to speak at all for a minute, and it needed two cups of indifferent coffee to loosen his tongue and soften the provocation of Mr Verity's muddled tirade. When it came, however, his story was short and clear.

At about five-forty-five on the morning of the murder, he had been standing at the window of his bedroom overlooking the square at the end of the street. It had been a sweltering night, and he had been quite unable to sleep. As he stood there breathing the cooler air from outside, a car came rattling down the street and drew to a stop near the post office. It was very light by this time, so that the vicar had been able to recognise the two men who got out of it. One was Winnidge; the other a newcomer to 'The Charter' whom description had since revealed to have been Maxwell.

"They were talking very loudly," Mr Robertson continued eagerly, "but I'm afraid I couldn't hear what they were saying!"

"But not for want of trying hard, I daresay," put in Verity.

"They had evidently chosen this place as the scene for some sort of quarrel. I think they were about to come to blows."

"What do you mean, you *think*?"

"Well, you see, at this moment my sister called me from her bedroom to ask what I was doing."

"You mean you left the window?"

"Well, yes, I must confess I did."

"Go on."

"When I came back, Mr Winnidge was carrying Mr Maxwell over his shoulder."

"You're sure it wasn't the other way about?" asked Verity.

"Quite sure. He put him beside him on the front seat, and then got in himself and drove off."

"Why didn't you report this before, sir?" asked Jackson.

"Well, you see, I had to go up to town yesterday. I only heard about the murder when I came back."

"And then?"

"Well, then came this tussle with my conscience I was telling you about. I mean—well, really it didn't seem right to—to give him away, did it?"

"I don't follow, sir."

"Well, after all, Mr Winnidge is one of my parishioners. He intends to settle here for good, so they say. Whereas this man Maxwell—"

"Was the stranger in your midst?" suggested Rambler.

"No, the devil in your midst," cried Verity. "Good for you, parson! Good for you! You're a fine fellow, do you hear?"

"Yes," said the little man bewilderedly. "I thought I was doing wrong."

"So you were," said Verity. "You were making Inspector Jackson's job a thousand times more difficult."

"Yes, so I realised. That's one of the reasons why I came round here in the end."

"And you were committing a crime by withholding information."

"Oh dear, I suppose I was."

"And you still haven't told us all we want to know," said Rambler. "For instance: was Mr Maxwell dead, do you think?"

"Oh, I really couldn't say."

"Did you hear a shot?"

"No, I did not."

"Did your sister?"

"No, she didn't either. She told me to come round here from the first—but I wasn't so sure. Matilda's always right…"

"You realise, sir," said Jackson, "that you might have been instrumental in sending an innocent man to the gallows?"

"Clichés, always clichés," said Verity to himself. Out loud he commended the vicar again with a "Have a cigar, parson."

"Thank you, no. Not at midday."

Verity frowned and lit up another for himself.

"But," Rambler pursued doggedly, "he did seem hurt?"

"Oh, yes, indeed. He looked unconscious to me, at the least. He may very well have been dead… Oh, dear—I do see how foolish I have been…"

"Never mind that now. Can you remember anything else?"

"Well, when he was put inside the car—by the driving seat—I recall that he fell forward against the front window."

"Did he, indeed?"

"Yes, I recall that distinctly."

"Good!" said Verity, rising precipitately. "There's no shooting without blood. Let us ring for a taxi."

Rambler rose too.

"I shall go and telephone," he said. "Thank you, vicar. You have been most helpful. I hope to see you later. As you are my host, Verity, you can take care of my meal."

Mr Verity paid reluctantly for his guest, and, on his own insistence, for Mr Robertson too. Then he showed the little man very courteously off the premises.

"Now I've done my duty by the Church," he said to Jackson, coming back into the lounge.

"Yes, Mr Verity."

"Incidentally, I don't think there's any use in picking up Winnidge yet. How would it be if Mr Rambler and myself just slipped down and gave him a preliminary interview?"

"As you please," said Jackson cheerfully. "I've got all my work cut out going over this stuff again. What was the girl telling you out there this morning?"

Verity told him.

"It's as I observed to you when first we met her, Jackson. She may easily have done it—for the best of noble reasons."

"Yes, sir." He fiddled with his empty coffee cup. "Inspector Rambler's set on this idea of an accomplice, isn't he?"

"Of course. Aren't you?"

"I suppose I am; it's the only way out, isn't it?"

"Well, then, why the hesitation?"

"It's nothing, sir. I was just thinking."

"Yes?"

Verity sat down again at the littered table. Jackson waited for Alice to clear off the dessert plates and the used tumblers before adding:

"About the Manageress."

"Miss Framer?"

"Yes. She's a woman with a past, if ever I saw one."

"Every woman like that has what you call a Past. Something which long ago shrivelled up the woman in her. That livid face-powder is a perverse kind of mourning for a departed femininity."

Jackson stared.

"I mean," he said, "that she had the opportunity and she probably had the motive."

"Oh, never mind the motive if she had the opportunity! Motives keep popping up all over the place here. The whole trouble is that so many people wanted to kill Maxwell, and so few could have done."

"Well, she had the opportunity, didn't she? She had the pass-key. That means that she could have killed Maxwell earlier on and then locked the door afterwards, and come downstairs again as if nothing had happened."

"You mean she knew all along that Maxwell was dead when Paxton came running down the stairs shouting 'Murder'?"

"Yes—why not?"

"And she only pretended to lose the pass-key?"

"Yes—so that she could plant it later under Cunningham's chair!" Jackson was clearly pleased with himself.

"It's an interesting line to work on," Verity agreed. "Of course you can't account for the presence of Miss Burton in the wardrobe."

"No, not at the moment. I suppose it does come back to the accomplice theory in the end."

"I think it does. Of course she and Miss Burton could have worked together—but it's an unlikely idea. There seems little point, either, in leaving her trussed up."

"No, there doesn't seem much," Jackson said moodily.

"And further: even if there were no waitress trussed up inside the wardrobe, there'd still be certain difficulties in the way. The gun, for instance, bears the prints of every suspect in the hotel—but unfortunately not hers."

"There could be another gun, sir," said Jackson, piqued at being so easily demolished.

"There could be," agreed the old man. "Search her room, if you like. But I doubt if you'll find anything of value. Besides, when a .45 revolver—recently fired—is found next to a corpse—recently dead—it is not unreasonable to suppose that revolver to be the murder weapon."

"No, sir," said Jackson, reddening.

"And remember that I was there in the hall when the news was told her. She fainted."

"That could have been a fake."

"It wasn't. She was evidently very shocked."

"None of that 'triumph' you saw on the other one?"

"Good Lord, no! She was just frightened. Afterwards she was probably very relieved indeed—because she's obviously involved somewhere."

"You mean she's covering up for Paxton?"

"Exactly. And if Paxton's confession is true—which it probably is—I think I'd be willing to bet on what that Past is."

Rambler joined them.

"I've just spoken to Winnidge:—said I was speaking from the Station."

"Well?"

"It's no use. He says the taxi's out of order."

"Excellent!" Verity rubbed his hands and rose.

"The Directory gives his address as Number 2 East Bay."

"That's between here and Carrington," said Jackson. "About three miles out of Amnestie."

"The walk will do us good," said Verity.

"Too hot," said Rambler.

"See you at supper."

The phone rang. Miss Framer was heard answering it in the hall.

"Yes? Just a minute. I'll fetch him." She put her head round the door and said sourly: "Mr Verity: it's the Press."

"What?"

"The papers want a statement."

"How ridiculous! No one keeps his mouth shut—that's the trouble!"

"Well, you didn't expect to leave it a secret, did you?" asked Miss Framer venomously. "It's all over the country by now!"

"There was something in this morning's *Yardstick*," added Rambler.

"Getting everything wrong, I suppose. Jackson, you didn't make any statement, did you?"

"No, sir, I did not. But I think we'd better tell them something."

"I'll not be badgered, Jackson."

"No, Mr Verity."

"He sounded very insistent," put in Miss Framer from the door.

"Oh, did he? Well he'll get nothing out of me! What rag does the fool represent? *The Yardstick*?"

"I couldn't make out. There was too much noise in the background."

Verity stormed into the hall.

"Well?"

"Mr Verity?"

"Well?"

"This is *The Yardstick*."

"Well?"

"What about a statement?"

"Who do you think I am? A clergyman?"

"What's that?"

"Do you expect me to issue a statement on high matters before I understand them myself?"

"That'll be fine…"

"I tell you, you newspaper men are the real dope-peddlers! It should be you we find locked up in cupboards and bleeding to death on carpets! Do you hear me?"

"And then what happened?…"

Mr Verity roared into the receiver.

"O.K.," said the man at the other end. "We'll send someone down."

The old man came back panting.

"Curiosity! Curiosity!… That's the trouble with people!… Even when I went down to the post office this morning there were big white faces watching me behind the curtains all along the street!"

"Well, you're going out now," said Rambler imperturbably. "Faces or no faces, we must see Winnidge this afternoon."

Mr Verity snorted, and plunged through the French window. Rambler followed him, more ponderously. The Inspector was left at the table, still unwilling to abandon Miss Framer as the chief suspect, and puzzling over the possible ways she could have murdered her victim without assistance.

It was a blazing afternoon. Mr Verity panted heavily as he flopped, rather than walked, down the steep hill towards Carrington; and Detective-Inspector Rambler groaned and slithered behind him. In this style they travelled in silence till the road levelled out. Then Rambler drew up with his friend and gazed at him admonishingly with his mournful eyes.

"You know," he said at last, "I don't understand a single word you say when you embark on one of your luncheon speeches. And yet you always get there in the end. I'll never understand that."

"It would be better if one could keep one's eyes shut in this case," said Verity sincerely. "It's like rinsing one's hands through slime. Take this interview with Winnidge—I know so much about him already! When I break him down, he'll tell me more, and all of it pathetic."

"How do you know so much about him?"

"I talked to his young lady this morning while you were bathing." For the second time that hour Verity recounted his interview with Alice. "That's why I want you to walk with me as far as the young man's house, and then let me go in alone."

"All right. As you please. If Jackson didn't mind our going without *him*, there's no reason why I should mind your going without *me*."

"None whatever, Porpoise. Of course Jackson thinks we're both going in, but somehow I feel the fewer the better. He'll prove much more difficult if we both go."

They were now on the coastal road, watching the water rolling beyond the white beach as if the sea itself were at anchor.

Rambler took the initiative.

"I confess," he said, "that I made a mistake. But I still think that the theory is right. After all, it's the only logical one."

"True," said Verity.

"Well, there are still two alternatives. Miss Burton could have done it by herself, or with an accomplice—only this time substitute Winnidge for Cunningham. Let us explain the vicar's story for the moment."

"And Mr Swabber's story."

"Who? Oh—yes, the man next door. Very well, let us say that all Winnidge administered to Maxwell was a knock-out blow with his fist. Remember there's been no talk of a gun, either by the vicar or Mr Swabber. A good smack with a fist would account for the collapsed figure in the car-seat; the blood found by ourselves at the foot of the stairs; and the moaning heard by Mr Swabber in the early hours of the morning."

"True again," said Verity. "And also the bruise Dr Pelham found on Maxwell's face."

"Very well, then, let us leave Maxwell, bruised but not shot, in his room from about six-thirty to seven-thirty. At this point he sends for his favourite waitress. Reluctantly she arrives—and, as she confessed to you, filled with more hatred than she had ever felt for anyone."

"That was the night before," said Verity.

"I don't imagine it had cooled much in the night," Rambler retorted.

"Well… I grant you that."

"And she takes with her the gun which she has stolen from Cunningham's room. After all, Cunningham may have been telling you the truth when he said he hadn't seen the gun on the morning of the murder."

"Even assuming he was telling the truth, there are still Paxton's prints on it to account for."

"That is not difficult to explain. He probably picked up the gun when he found Maxwell's body."

"Go on."

"Maxwell, say, tries to embrace Miss Burton. They quarrel violently, and in the quarrel Alice shoots him. It is not a fatal wound, and he lurches round the room, spilling the blood we found, till she summons up the courage to fire again. He drops dead instantaneously. At this moment she sees a man outside on the balcony. It is Paxton. Quickly she hides—in the wardrobe—as Paxton climbs in. He sees Maxwell's body, picks up Cunningham's gun which she has inadvertently left on the floor, and bolts. Now she steals out again and makes to follow him quickly out of the room—when another noise is heard at the very door she is about to open."

"Good," said Verity. "Cunningham."

"Yes. Back she goes to her wardrobe. Cunningham comes in to 'reason' with Maxwell, as he said, sees the body and—terrified of being seen coming out of the murdered man's door—flees through the window."

"You are suggesting we believe Cunningham's story in its entirety."

"There's nothing against it."

"True."

"Well, then she panics. She rushes to the door and locks it. She darts over to the window—there below is Cunningham in the arms of a policeman. An idea occurs to her. Why not blame the whole thing on to him?... The story of the masked man is still the invention of a moment: no one will ever convince me otherwise."

"Well?"

"So she ties her legs up inside the cupboard, shutting the door upon herself. But her mistakes were obvious: if she realised them she did so too late. For one thing she had left the gun on the floor."

"Perhaps she meant to leave it there," said Verity, "as part of her plan to incriminate Cunningham. Perhaps she forgot that her own prints were also on it."

"That's very likely. Or perhaps she just forgot to get rid of it." He stopped, badly out of breath. "Let's sit here a minute and rest."

The two fat men halted at a cliff-top and lowered themselves precariously into the long grass. Below them children, in bright-coloured trunks, were running about on the sand.

"But her biggest mistake was in locking the door and the window," Rambler resumed presently. "She did that, of course, before she thought up her story of the man in the mask. Unfortunately for her, that action in itself is sufficient proof that she wasn't tied up by any murderer."

Verity cut off the heads of several dandelions and dropped them over the side of the cliff. They were received with shrieks of delight below.

"There's just one thing, Porpoise," he said, waving to the children. "I grant you that Winnidge knocked out Maxwell: it seems a very likely explanation. I grant you that the story of the mask is pretty fantastic. But one thing rather confirms it."

"What's that?"

"I mean the key of the wardrobe on the inside of the door."

"What about it?"

"Certainly any man locking a woman in for a certain space of time would put the key in with her, where she could find it easily. He would only want time to make his get-away. He had no interest in keeping her imprisoned for long. What more natural than he should put the key in with her? Or that a woman inventing such a story would forget a minute detail like that?"

"A good point, but not sufficient to shake the story. She is a clever woman—"

"Resourceful, anyway—"

"And she obviously remembered to put the key beside her as a convincing detail."

"A woman clever enough to remember a tiny detail like that—clever enough to believe we would think her too stupid to be capable of such a thing—would *not* make the obvious mistakes she did. She would *not* lock the door. She would *not* lock the window. And she would either have hidden the gun after using it, or put on gloves in the first place."

Verity stood up, and offered a hand to his friend.

"You are wrong, Porpoise," he said. "You are wrong."

Let us then try the second of my alternatives, said Rambler, not a whit shaken.

"That she was an accomplice of Winnidge?"

"Yes."

"I can think of nothing more likely," said Verity. "However, unless I'm mistaken, that's Winnidge's house over there, Number 2, East Bay."

He pointed to a neat house whose blue gables faced the sea above windows which glittered in the sunlight.

"I like that house," said Verity. "Markedly inconspicuous."

Adjoining it was a garage in which they could see the back of a capacious car. There was no one about.

"Let's go and see what's wrong with it," said Rambler.

"No, I will," said Verity. "You sit over there."

Rambler looked at him sulkily for a moment, and then sighed.

"Very well. I'll be under that tree when you're finished. It's far too hot to sit in the open." He made off into the shade of a large conifer and Verity crossed the road to the house Then, as noiselessly as he could, he approached the garage.

It was a large car, capable of taking seven in comfort. The left-hand door, opposite the driving-seat, was open; a bucket of soapy water stood on the floor. Mr Verity entered the garage on tip-toe and peered gingerly in at the open door. The seat, sure enough, was damp where it had been recently washed: darker spots showed through on the wide patch of wet seating. Mr Verity nodded in satisfaction.

"Yes?" said a harsh voice.

He turned. At the entrance of the garage a man of about thirty stood regarding him: his white shirt dazzled in the sunlight. Beyond his shoulder Mr Verity could see Rambler, apparently asleep under the tree, on the other side of the road.

"Mr Edward Winnidge?"

"Yes."

"My name is Verity."

"I know."

"Oh!"

"I've seen you poking your nose into things before now. What were you after this time?"

"Blood," said Verity. "Is there anywhere we can talk?"

"This is good enough for me."

"As you please."

"That's always supposing I want to talk."

"I think it'd be best if you did. You're not in a very enviable position."

The man came closer. He had a clumsy jaw and large ears, but was not bad-looking in an averagely sensual way.

"Meaning what?" he said.

Mr Verity hitched up his flannels and sat down very deliberately on the running-board.

"There are certain things I ought to explain," he said. "Your fiancée is in serious trouble."

"Alice?"

"There's absolutely no use squaring your jaw at me, Mr Winnidge. I know too much for that sort of treatment to be really effective. You say you know me. Very well, you know that I am concerned in the investigation of Mr Maxwell's murder."

"Mr Maxwell!" Winnidge spat fiercely. "And you want me to help?"

"I'm afraid I do. Don't imagine I like doing this:—what I have gleaned about Maxwell in only a few hours has convinced me that his death was an unalleviated benefit for a great many people."

"Why investigate it, then?"

"Interest, Mr Winnidge. Interest wedded to duty. The case intrigues me as no case has ever done before. There are so many possible answers:—and most of them hinge on Alice. That's why you must answer my questions. I am not asking you to help hang Maxwell's murderer—but to help Alice clear herself with the police."

"How can *I* help? Did she send you here?"

"I think she knows I'd be here some time. You see, she told me a great deal."

Winnidge bent down and started polishing the car with a rag.

"What do you want to know?"

"A few answers. You were in the habit of taking Maxwell for late night drives?"

"Yes, I took him—but I didn't know it was him. If only I had!... If only!..."

"Perhaps it was just as well you didn't," observed Verity, watching the dirty water stream out of the rag he was squeezing between his large hands. "On the night before he was murdered, did you take him out?"

There was a faint hesitation before he replied:

"Yes. He phoned for me about four in the morning."

"Didn't you object to being called out so late?"

"It wasn't usually as late as that—and it always meant a few quid. And that night, you see, I knew."

"You mean Alice had told you that Maxwell was down here, and pestering her?"

"Yes. She'd told me earlier on. And so I went. I picked him up about four-thirty."

"Did anyone see you?"

"No one I can think of. I was pretty quiet, of course. And I fancy most of them were asleep."

"Naturally. Go on."

"I drove him around for an hour or so. I think he enjoyed sitting in the back, making me drive him about. He didn't say a word to me. But I felt him watching me all the time. I kept on driving—trying to keep myself under control, I suppose. He didn't guess anything. In the end I stopped the car. Then I told him I knew."

"Where was this?"

"Amnestie Square—at the end of the High Street."

"Are you sure it was there?"

"Of course I'm sure. I made him get out. He was scared stiff, and never took his eyes off me. I told him to pack his bags and get out on the first train. He just stood and looked at me—and then he laughed. I remember he laughed… like a woman!"

"And then?"

"I took a swipe at him. He fell and hit his face on the side of the mudguard. He split his cheek open and the blood ran all down his face. There was some coming from his mouth as well."

"What did you do?"

"He was out cold. I picked him up and slung him back into the car beside me, and took him back to the hotel. I had to carry him upstairs to his room."

"Did anyone see you?" asked Verity, watching the man's face carefully. It was possible that the vicar had made himself as conspicuous to Winnidge as Winnidge had to the vicar.

"No one," said Winnidge decisively. "Oh, wait! There was someone in the hall. I remember I stood and chatted to him for a minute at the foot of the stairs."

"Oh? Who was this?"

"Some odd chap up at the hotel. I've taken him to the station a couple of times."

"Didn't he think it rather peculiar that you should be standing talking to him with a body slung over your shoulder?"

"Well, it's as I say—he's odd himself, so he wouldn't take much notice of it. I think he even expected it—talked a lot about plots and conspiracies and suchlike."

"Really? Do you happen to know his name?"

"Tudor. Richard Rudor, I think. He's quite a character round here. He thinks he's the King, so they tell me. But harmless."

"What did you tell him?"

"I told him the truth," said Winnidge levelly. "I told him we'd had a fight. Maxwell came round then and started hollering—so I had to get him upstairs."

"And then?"

"I left him on the bed, and went out of his room."

"You saw Alice?"

"No, I didn't. I just walked around for a bit, then went home. The first I heard of him being dead was in 'The Bellows' at lunch-time. And that's the truth, so help me."

"Yes, I think it is."

"What's that?"

"I said I think it is the truth—so far as it goes. But I preferred to have it from you."

"Here… I don't understand."

"There's no need that you should. When did you last see Alice?"

He hesitated.

"Last night," he said finally. "I had to see if she was all right. So I walked up and threw pebbles at her window till she came down. We went into the garden."

"I see. Then you must realise what an uncomfortable situation she is in."

"Situation? I don't know that I do. Her story's alright to me."

"You're naturally prejudiced," Verity smiled. But Winnidge's eyes blazed angrily.

"You mean you don't believe her?"

"Shall I say that at the moment the facts don't permit me to?"

"Here—that's enough of that! What Alice says is the living truth—no matter how funny it sounds!…"

"I see she told it all to you last night."

"Yes, that's right. She did."

"Or did you tell it all to her the night before?"

There was a sudden pause. Winnidge had turned ghastly pale.

"What?" The man's voice was hoarse and his hands were trembling. "What are you trying to say?… You don't believe my story?… Why don't you ask that looney Tudor?… Well?…"

"Your story has a more respectable witness than that," said Verity, getting up and dusting himself carefully. "I have a minister of the Gospel to vouch for your act of violence in the square at Amnestie."

Winnidge gaped at him and sweat broke out on his face. Mr Verity walked past him, and then he stopped.

"Don't take me for a fool," he said quietly. "Good afternoon. And I shall always be interested in any story of yours—even when it comes through the mouth of your fiancée."

CHAPTER IX

ALL THE WAY ACROSS THE DUSTY ROAD OVER THE GRASS to the conifer tree, all the time he stirred Rambler with his foot and helped him to rise, Mr Verity felt the maddened stare of Winnidge resting on him.

"Not guilty?" asked Rambler sleepily.

"Not innocent, at any rate of desire. The capacity of this young couple for righteous hatred is really amazing—it compels my admiration. When he spoke about hitting Maxwell, there was a look on his face—like a crusader who had just skewered Saladin."

"Then he did hit Maxwell, as I suggested?"

"Yes. Hence the bruise on the face and the blood in the hall. Hence, too, the vicar's story."

Verity recounted the whole interview. When he had finished, Rambler nodded with pleasure.

"Good. I see you incline to my alternative solution, which we were about to discuss just before arriving here."

"That the two were accomplices? Yes. Where logic leads we needs must follow."

"Substitute, as I said, Winnidge for Cunningham—"

"Let's substitute them in a tea-shop," said Verity, dabbing at his forehead.

They quickened their steps into Amnestie.

'The Lantern' was a tiny, stifling room, crowded with small circular tables on which the waitress had placed uniform cloths of yellow-check, salt and pepper in cellars, oil and vinegar in bottles, mustard in egg-cups, and shiny plates reading 'The Thistle, Morecombe'.

"Such parsimony defeats me," declared Verity. "There is nothing more disenchanting than auction-bought china. What are you having?"

They had the set tea. This cost two shillings, and was mainly little triangular sandwiches filled artfully with lettuce. Through the windows they could see the doors of 'The Bellows' firmly closed until evening.

"Ridiculous!" snorted Verity. "No one needs to drink in the evening—except a mellow handful of old fisher-folk. Alcohol in the afternoon is the most infallible cure for things I know."

Rambler said nothing, but started rummaging in the cake-plate.

"Besides, I want to go into that particular pub just as soon as it opens. Winnidge claims to have been in there when he first heard the news of the murder."

"He probably was," said Rambler.

"I want to know how he took it. Mellow handsful of fisher-folk make amazingly accurate observers of that sort of thing."

A selection from 'The Chocolate Soldier' came softly through the loud-speaker. The two detectives lit cigars and had soon almost vanished in the smoke. 'The Lantern' began to look, as well as feel, like a Turkish Bath, and the waitress choked as she cleared away.

"You were substituting Winnidge for Cunningham," prompted Verity.

"So I was. You see, the first thing we do must be to find an accomplice for Alice. That is the only logical answer."

"Well?"

"Let us take the evidence as we now have it. Alice did the locking-up, but, for reasons you gave me earlier on this afternoon, it is unlikely that she was acting on her own initiative."

"Exactly. No one could have been at once so clever about small details and so stupid about big ones."

"No one, you mean, acting on her own. But look at this thing as the work of an accomplice and it all becomes comprehensible."

"I think it does."

"Of course it does. It's fairly obvious that some pre-arranged plan was carried out in Maxwell's bedroom. It is also fairly obvious that the plan was bungled. As Dr Pelham pointed out to us last night at dinner, it is difficult to think of criminals bungling things quite as we do in ordinary life. Now why was this plan bungled? Why? I'll tell you. Because it was not properly mastered."

"You mean that the plan was the invention of Winnidge?"

"Exactly. Invented by Winnidge and carried out by his Alice. Now look at his story:—it can be right in every particular but one. That is, he could have shot Maxwell in that square, and not just socked him on the jaw."

"Aren't you forgetting that Tudor met him in the hall? According to Winnidge Maxwell came round as they were talking."

"I said shot—not killed. He shot him again when he found that his first bullet had merely wounded him. He obviously had a silencer on his gun—that was why neither the vicar nor the vicar's sister, nor Mr Swabber nor Mr Paxton heard the shot. Later he could have tossed it into the sea."

"That certainly fits in with Swabber's story of hearing someone fall on to the floor next door, and then there being silence. Up to that time there had been moaning, remember."

"I do remember!" said Rambler, rubbing his hands with glee. "Shall I go on?"

"But of course. One thing worries me, I must confess. A man you shoot in the back is apt to bleed rather profusely. We only found a small stain of blood at the foot of the stairs."

"It is not inevitable that he would bleed profusely," said Rambler, reaching through the tobacco-smoke for another éclair. "However, we might be able to verify that with your Mr Tudor."

"That's if he's still on speaking terms with me. It must have been pretty dark in the vestibule all the same."

"True, but he may be able to tell us something of interest. Anyway, let me proceed. After killing him properly, Winnidge creeps up to Alice's room and gives his instructions. Remember again that Mr Swabber gives fifteen minutes as the interval between the door closing and the car starting up; and Winnidge himself says he walked about before going home. What does he say he was doing?"

"Thinking," said Verity.

"Well, he was, of course—and quickly. I suspect she must have told him about Cunningham's gun—and that set him thinking. He knew the evidence against him was pretty strong, didn't he?"

"Did he?"

"Well, apart from what Tudor had seen, he knew that Maxwell might have that letter of his, warning him to leave Alice alone. He obviously tried to find it that night—you may recall how our invaluable Swabber heard someone going noisily round the bedroom. I should say the mess we found there resulted at least in part from his frantic search."

"That sounds reasonable."

"You see, he wasn't to know that others, actually in the hotel, were involved with Maxwell as deeply as he was."

"He must have guessed Cunningham was, when he heard about his arriving with a gun."

"Yes I think he must. And that started something in his mind."

"You mean he told Alice to steal Cunningham's gun and put it beside the corpse?"

"Exactly. She must have stolen it while he was sleeping. There wasn't much time."

"Amazing!"

"It took a certain amount of nerve, I agree."

"She has it," said Verity shortly.

"Oh yes, she has it. And she needed it to do what she had to do. You can be sure that the wardrobe was his idea. He told her to tie her ankles up inside it, probably showed her how to make a convincing knot. The object was simple enough: it wasn't sufficient that Cunningham's gun be found in the room by the dead man's side. Oh no—it would be far better if Miss Burton were there to testify that Cunningham was on the scene in person."

"It was subtle not letting her identify him until she had heard him speak."

"Very subtle. It made it look far less like a deliberate attempt to incriminate him."

"How very amusing!" said Verity, beating Rambler by a finger's length to the last jam-tart. "Miss Burton sits in a wardrobe by a dead man's side preparing to testify that she saw a man kill him. All of a sudden that man walks through the door."

"No, first Paxton appeared. *Then* Cunningham."

"Sorry, I was forgetting Paxton. It was quite a busy morning in the Maxwell bedroom."

"It certainly was. She must have been terrified. That's why, after her second visitor, she locked the door and the window. Panic always seems to overcome these women accomplices at the last moment. If only she'd left them alone!"

"And kept her own prints off the gun!"

"Yes, nothing can excuse that. It was just a piece of down-right stupidity."

"I excuse it," said Verity. "It is helping you to solve a murder."

"I don't like give-aways," said Rambler peevishly. "And that's exactly what this is. The whole plan was bungled from start to finish. It was not a bad plan, as plans go: but unfortunately Winnidge had to rely on its being carried out by someone who didn't quite understand what she was doing."

"I don't think that."

"Well, someone who couldn't keep all the little details in her head at any rate. That's why she remembered to put the key in the wardrobe beside her, for example, but yet made such dreadful bloomers with the pistol and the window. Fragments of the plan were done right—but most of it was hopelessly botched in the panic of the moment."

"The whole thing is pleasingly Greek," said Verity after a pause. "We can only understand Plato's conception of the material world if we view it as an imperfect copy of an ideal original; like Plato, we have glimpsed an ideal plan through the distortion of its bungled copy."

"But Plato," said Rambler, getting up, "had the whole world to supply him with distorted evidence for the existence of his undistorted plan: we have only a small bedroom. It is a thousand pities that we have to guess so much."

The waitress, still choking from the cigar-smoke, presented the bill. They had consumed eleven cakes between them.

At the door of 'The Lantern' they parted. 'The Bellows' had just opened and one or two of the town's thirsty were already straggling towards its door. Detective Inspector Rambler went to slake with them, and find out what he could about the reactions of Ted Winnidge to the news of Maxwell's death. Mr Verity, meanwhile, went slowly back to 'The Charter'.

He found Jackson sitting over a late tea by the pool in the garden. At the other end, nearest the hotel, some of the old ladies who peopled its upper storeys were grouped together on little canvas chairs, engaged in subdued speculation. Under the apple-tree Colonel Rainchart was snoozing fitfully, and among the thick flower-beds behind him his dashed little puppy was sneezing distressedly into the pollinic air.

"Excellent!" said Verity, sitting down beside him and eyeing the Swiss Rolls. "I'll join you!" The deck-chair bulged dangerously beneath him.

"Had a good time?" asked Jackson.

"Solved the case, nigh-on," said Verity.

Over his second tea the old man narrated the events of the afternoon in careful sequence, from the time when he had entered Winnidge's garage to the recent parting from Rambler.

"So he thinks it's a partnership, does he?"

"It's what the evidence adds up to."

"I suppose it is," said Jackson slowly. "I suppose it is."

He seemed a little stupefied by the sun, and was watching the silver fish which still within their water-circle wandered through reflected branches.

"Has anything fresh occurred here?"

"Nothing but a whole crowd of journalists from London asking for you. I gave them some of the story and let them take a few photos. It was the least I could do."

"Rabble!" The light of battle kindled again in the old man's eye. "I wish I had been there! I really wish…"

"And I interviewed Mr Paxton again."

"About the prints on the gun?"

"Yes. I asked him to describe all his movements to me after he had climbed through that window. He confessed he'd picked up the weapon out of curiosity, without thinking what he was doing. Of course he dropped it again pretty quickly once it had sunk in. Or so he says."

"Do you believe him?"

Jackson looked pleadingly at the old man.

"It's easiest to, isn't it?"

"Much. And there's nothing really lazy-minded about it, either. Paxton's fairly well down on my list of suspects. The person who did this had an accomplice. One must always keep fast to that."

"Yes. Paxton's out as far as I can see."

"And now you must excuse me," said Verity. "I'll join you at 'The Bellows' in about half-an-hour. It is most urgent that I see Mr Tudor."

"Mr Tudor?" Jackson stared foolishly.

"Yes. It sounds a dreadful prospect, I admit, but what can I do? After all, he may be able to tell us whether Maxwell had a bruise on his jaw or a bullet in his back in the small hours of Wednesday morning. It's just possible he may have seen."

"Yes, but—but—"

There was a look of alarm on the Inspector's normally placid face, which Verity did not fail to catch.

"Whatever's the matter?" he demanded brusquely, pulling himself out of his deck-chair and standing upright. "It's a perfectly routine business."

"Yes, but don't you see, Mr Verity—he's disappeared!"

"He's—what?"

"There were several phone calls for him this afternoon, but no one could find him anywhere. Of course I didn't give it much thought, but now—"

"Now he has become a most important witness. Nay, a vital witness!"

"I understand that, sir. I never imagined such a thing."

"No more did I. When was he last seen?"

"Miss Framer says he wasn't at lunch. Apparently we were the last to see him in here this morning."

"I saw him after that. We walked down to the post office and back. But where did he go after that? Damn it, he *can't* have disappeared!"

"Well, no one can find him—which amounts to the same thing," said Jackson, rising too.

"No, it doesn't at all!" said Verity sharply. He was plainly discomposed. "There is always tragedy about people who disappear. People whom 'no one can find' are a very different matter altogether: they're always quite safely developing photographs or playing the organ somewhere. Mr Tudor is just the kind of man to do both."

"Yes," said Jackson doubtfully. "He'll probably turn up for supper as if nothing has happened."

"Nothing *will* have happened!" shouted Verity with more insistence than conviction. "I tell you he's tracing pedigrees somewhere as happily as can be!"

A blended murmur of curiosity and disquietude arose from the other end of the garden. Mr Verity moderated his tone.

"He'd better be," he said, and stumped off into the hotel.

Once in the lounge he hesitated. The cool within afforded intense relief from the glare of the open, and he was tempted to sit in one of the green velvet armchairs and thumb through half a dozen 'Spheres' before supper. And yet, pleasant as it was there, the old man could not stay at ease. He felt puzzled and restless, and vaguely conscious that what he really needed was a long, hard think in a darkened room. He wandered out into the hall, then into the street: it was deserted and beautiful in the rich light of a gathered summer evening. He went back to the hotel, but the hall was empty: Miss Framer was nowhere to be seen. He had just settled himself in the lounge when Colonel Rainchart marched in from the garden, his little dog under his arm.

"Excuse me," said Verity, "but have you seen Mr Tudor?"

The Colonel barked; so did the dog.

"Mr Tudor!… Everyone wants Mr Tudor! As if *I'd* have seen him! Shouldn't be surprised if they'd taken him away, that's what! Not a bit surprised!"

He passed stiffly out of sight. Mr Verity sighed and reached for a 'Sphere'. There was the picture of a hapless sea-diver, a Mr Mayne-Allison, clambering up the side of a ship out of the Yellow Sea. Underneath, Mr Mayne-Allison was quoted as saying, *"Believe me, the octopus is really the friend of man."*

Outside the insects were buzzing tirelessly. Mr Verity yawned and put down the magazine: he was more oppressed than ever by the thought that somewhere, not too far away, lay a solution to this tangled business. Rambler's theory was logically right; everything pointed to its being the only answer; and yet it was somehow too ingenious to fit the case. Alice and her Ted were simple people: they would murder in a simple way. Any crime of theirs—and they were perfectly capable of doing murder several times over—would be straightforward and passionate: neither would have the wit or the desire to coil so subtle a skein of deceit about the deed. Yet it was obvious that some sort of plan had been adopted... And, because they were both simple people, it was likely that some details of it had been written down—at any rate by her. There was just a chance that in Alice's bedroom something... some small scrap...

Mr Verity rose at once and, throwing a quick glance round, mounted the stairs swiftly, and on tip-toe. The corridors were deserted as he passed the landings, and noises, barely audible, came from behind bedroom doors: the gentle replacing of tea-things by elderly, orderly hands; the routine and wasted toilet in preparation for the evening-meal. The maids slept on the top floor, and Alice's room—as Matthews had told him— was the last on the right. Here reigned absolute silence—save for his own heavy panting from the long toil up: evidently the maids had already smartened themselves and departed to lay the tables. Nevertheless, the old man stood listening several minutes outside her door before he knocked. He was gratified by receiving no reply. Quickly he ventured in and shut the door. Now that he was actually inside the room, the curious conviction that something of profit could be gained from a personal search, evaporated: he was left feeling rather foolish in the middle of the tiny, shabby room. By this time, of course, any written plan of campaign, any list of points to be remembered, must surely have been destroyed...

A sudden instinct made him peer under the pillow. Of course there was nothing there. He moved to the window and stared down into the garden, at the hump-backed apple tree in the failing light. Only last night, on his own confession, Winnidge had stood below this window and tossed up pebbles. (He probably thought he had been seen, or he would never have confessed to it.) She had gone down to him, trembling in her dressing-gown down all those flights of stairs: she had met him in the garden and told him all that had happened. How they must have panicked—out there in the dark, warm night!... What had they said to each other, those hard-faced lovers?

"Destroy everything," he had whispered. "At once— destroy everything."

And of course she had. There was no use looking for anything here. Idly he turned away and opened the first drawer of the dressing-table. It smelt of face powder. There were stockings, handkerchiefs, hundreds of hair-pins. He rummaged through it slowly. Ribbons... bottles... a shawl... a spare cap—or was it a cap? It was square and black and showed two large holes which had been pushed through the silk. He raised the thing carefully to his face and looked at himself with amusement in the cracked mirror.

For the first time in his life his beard looked absolutely right. But then it was the first time Mr Verity had seen himself in a mask.

CHAPTER X

"IT'S ALL PERFECTLY PLAIN NOW," SAID RAMBLER HEAVily. "She was either going to plant this on Cunningham, or say she found it in his room."

It was nine-thirty. They were sitting in the lounge eating dinner as they had eaten lunch, away from the hotel guests. There had been no other new developments, save that the regulars at 'The Bellows' had more or less confirmed the details of Winnidge's story.

Alice came in with the coffee. Verity thought she looked at him with unusual sharpness. They all stopped talking and waited in embarrassment while she poured out.

"And then there's Tudor," Rambler pursued as the door shut. "What the devil can have happened to him?"

"I don't know, sir," said Jackson seriously. "Nothing good, I'm sure."

"Well, he must be found! And at once!"

"I've sent out warnings, sir. There's nothing else we can do for the moment."

Rambler grunted.

"All is very far from being well there. People don't just disappear like that—especially such vitally important people."

"Do you suspect anyone, sir?"

"Winnidge," said Rambler shortly.

"You forget," said Mr Verity, "that Mr Winnidge himself told me about meeting Tudor. There was no need for him to have mentioned it."

"It could have slipped out unintentionally. Or maybe he had a purpose in talking."

"But he couldn't have had the time, sir," said Jackson. "Mr Verity left Tudor just before lunch and saw Winnidge just after."

"Until we know what he has done," said Rambler judicially, "we can hardly say whether he had time for it or not."

"No, sir," said Jackson, reddening as he always did at even the mildest rebuke.

"Besides, aren't you forgetting he has an accomplice?"

"No!" said Verity in genuine horror. "Impossible! She would never do such a thing!"

"I am accusing nobody of anything," said Rambler imperturbably. "I merely said he had an accomplice. Between them, Tudor could have been disposed of quite easily—at any rate for the moment."

"Yes. And their safety really would be endangered if what he saw… Oh, it's a horrible business!"

"Horrible, indeed."

"Then let's talk about something else. It's been a most crowded day."

Jackson nodded agreement.

"I can hardly believe this is only the second day we've been at it."

"Speed has always been the Verity watchword," said Rambler.

"And thoroughness the Porpoise," Verity replied.

Miss Framer came in carrying an evening paper. She was very angry.

"Here!" she said, brandishing it furiously above the table. "Just look at this! It's disgraceful!"

"Is it?" said Verity excitedly. "Let me see it! Oh, yes…"

He unfolded the paper eagerly and called out the headlines:

"'THE MYSTERY OF THE WOMAN IN THE WARDROBE!'… Excellent phrase! These men really have a flair for the language!"

Jackson looked dumbfounded.

"The hotel will never survive it," put in Miss Framer bitterly. "Never!"

"Nonsense. It'll be the making of it. You've risen in the world, don't you see? Before this, the most you got was a mention in some squalid divorce proceedings, but now—now there will be columns about you: about your delightful grounds, your perfect food, your charming residents… I assure you, Miss Framer, any place I treat with achieves immediate and lasting recognition. Three gentlemen of Ankara were once found with their throats cut in a lodging-house at Marseilles. It was solely because of my investigation that it became thereafter the Mecca of all men of taste who are forced to spend a night in that port."

Miss Framer bridled: "I hardly think—"

"Ah! Wait!… Look here!" He dived into the paper once more. "'RAMBLER AND VERITY TOGETHER AGAIN.'… Together again! 'This afternoon the two old hands were hard at work *interviewing suspected persons in the neighbourhood... Inspector Jackson, who is in charge of the case, said "I'm very proud to be working with two such famous men."'* Oh, Jackson!"

Inspector Jackson turned a bright scarlet and studied the carpet.

"'*The Charter of Amnestie, for ever associated in the public mind with the sensational divorce trials of Mrs Elsie Carruthers and Lady Enid Watts...*'"

"Has Mr Tudor returned?" asked Rambler hastily.

"No, he has not! And while we're on this subject"—her eyes sparked dangerously—"I should prefer it if Mr Verity did not take my waitress for walks in the garden when there is work to be done in the hotel."

"Perhaps," said Verity, looking up from his paper, "you would prefer me to take you instead?"

"How dare you!"

"I feel there is a great deal to be gained from such an expedition."

"Attempts to incriminate other people in murder," added Rambler levelly, "are not viewed with favour by the police."

Miss Framer took a step back and stared at them horrified.

"I don't understand."

"We found only your finger-prints on that pass-key," said Verity.

"Whose else did you want us to find?" asked Rambler.

"Perhaps we shouldn't ask Miss Framer leading questions."

"I suggest those of Mr Cunningham."

"No," cried Miss Framer. "I didn't... It was a mistake!"

"It certainly was."

"I never meant any harm by it. I swear I never meant any harm!…"

"I think you did, Miss Framer."

"I didn't know what I was doing!" She turned her head tirelessly from one to the other, like an enthusiastic spectator at a tennis match. "You must believe that! I didn't realise…"

"As I recall it," said Rambler quietly, "you made several rather clumsy attempts to cover up for Mr Paxton. There is no need to go over them now—but clumsiness seems to be the dominant note among criminals in this part of the world."

"Criminals!"

"Yes, criminals. An attempt to mislead the police such as yours I regard as criminal."

"And so is an attempt to lie to them," said Verity. "I remember distinctly that you told me the meeting between Mr Paxton and Mr Maxwell was very cordial—when it couldn't have been anything of the sort."

"And, above all, you denied knowing the late Mr Maxwell apart from his being a guest in your hotel. That, I submit, was a flat untruth."

Miss Framer opened her mouth several times and, standing between the two seated detectives, finally began crying: the tears blobbed out and fell heavily, fretting cadent channels in her powdered cheeks.

"I didn't mean any harm," she kept on saying.

"We are not interested in your past, or even your present relationship with Mr Paxton," said Verity simply. "At any rate, not for the moment. I know that years ago Mr Paxton helped you out of a—a difficulty. It cost him his professional career. You, I suppose, regarded it as incumbent on you to take a risk for his sake." Miss Framer resumed her idiotic mouthing. "What he did for you was done out of a mistaken sense of kindness—just as what you did for him was done out of a mistaken sense of loyalty. It threw needless obstacles in the way of the police and caused them to waste valuable time on irrelevancies. I therefore advise you, as strongly as I possibly can, never to try anything like it again."

"I—I—never…"

"Or you will find yourself in prison," added Rambler. "You are an infernal nuisance!"

"What?…"

"Now leave us."

"And take some of that powder off your face. At least some of what's done can be undone!"

For a moment Miss Framer stood undecisive at their table, torn between contrition at her actions and indignation at those of the police. Then she passed shuddering from the room; her sobs were heard in the hall.

"I should have realised before," said Verity ruminatively, "that when she fainted in the vestibule she wasn't thinking of Maxwell, but of what Paxton might have done to him."

"All the same," said Jackson approvingly, "you were right when you told me the other day you thought she was Paxton's old client."

Verity smiled.

"It was pretty obvious, really."

"Still quite a leap in the dark, sir."

"Well, let's get back to Miss Burton," said Rambler. "This discovery of the mask is, as I say, rather damning evidence."

"It certainly strengthens the case against her," said Jackson gravely.

"How odd!" said Verity, getting up and lighting a cigar. "I was just thinking how much it lightened it."

"What!"

"Indeed, yes. I think this mask is the most complicating thing we have met yet. But, as I have said before, we have had a tiring day. It is time to leave off work." He strolled over to the open French window. "It was nice being able to despatch Miss Framer."

"For tonight, at any rate," said Jackson.

"Ah!… So you still have your suspicions of her! I admit she's an unlovely person."

"She's more than that," said Rambler. "Where are you going?"

"Home. Home to my statues. I'm still labelling the smaller busts. You can help me if you like—I'm going by way of the beach."

"Oh, very well."

Rambler heaved himself to his feet and lumberingly followed his friend.

"Good night, Jackson," said Verity. "We'll see you in the morning."

"Good night, sir."

"If I were you I'd go straight to bed."

"Yes, sir."

The twilight dimmed and swallowed them.

. . .

At 'Persepolis' they found Dr Pelham waiting for them. He was sitting on a high stool in the living-room and, with his head on one side and his pince-nez gleaming in the candle-light, he looked rather like a parrot—a parrot with gold teeth that shone when he made a joke.

"I positively refuse to discuss the case," said Verity. "If you want to, you can have it out with Porpoise and I'll go into the garden."

"No," said Rambler. "*I'll* go into the garden. Excuse me, Doctor."

He inclined his vast body politely and went through the far door.

"Amazing!" said Pelham, looking after him admiringly. "He never lets it rest, does he?"

"Not till he's finished it. But I'm afraid he won't finish it tonight."

"Oh? What makes you so sure?"

"Because he has forgotten a piece in the jig-saw puzzle."

"One of your psychological factors, I suppose?"

"Oh no, something much more commonplace than that. But I don't want to tell him now because I'm preparing a little surprise for the morrow."

He poured out two glasses of port and, handing one to the doctor, sat down heavily. The statues looked down from their pedestals with chilling indifference.

"I hear you've been talking to our vicar," said Pelham. "You seem to have confused him terribly."

"How odd! I didn't mean to. I was only telling him what

I told Tudor earlier on—by the way, the vicar hasn't disappeared, has he?"

Dr Pelham looked blank.

"Not that I know of. What did you say to upset him?"

"Oh, just some stuff about old authority giving place to new—or rather to none at all."

"The 'none at all' bothered him, of course. It's a favourite jeremiad of clergymen."

"Exactly. That's why I'm surprised to hear that I confused the vicar. I'm afraid Mr Tudor took it even worse. I told *him* that the people's mandate had made *me* the power in the land."

"I suppose that's true," said Pelham after a moment, cocking his head on one side. "Of course we doctors are even luckier in that respect: we wield control all the time."

"Some of you do, at any rate. I hear the air is rather too good in Amnestie for you personally to exercise much power."

"Unfortunately that's true. All the same, I still manage to make myself indispensable to the healthy. Take old Mrs Treacher, for instance."

"Mrs Treacher?"

"An oldish woman who lives here. There is absolutely nothing the matter with her but indolence. She lay in bed for two months and did nothing but eat chocolates and read American magazines. In fact she was enjoying herself hugely until she made the mistake of calling me in."

"Why did she do that?"

"Because it is still *de rigueur* to call in a doctor to justify one's idleness. And once I was called in I had my own way entirely. Just because I was a doctor—and she hadn't even personally checked up on that—I could inflict any indignity and any inconvenience upon her."

"And did you?"

"Certainly I did. First I forbad her chocolates. Then I refused her all the pillows she had been propping herself against. That meant she had to lie against the iron bedstead to read. But she had put herself so completely into my hands that even that didn't make her rebel."

"It's amazing!"

"Yes, indeed. After a time I told her reading was affecting her metabolism and that she would have to give it up. There was a little struggle over that—but of course she lost."

"What happened then?"

"She just lay there. Nothing I did could make her get up on her own initiative. In the end I had to lance her."

"What?"

"In the behind. Then I told her she was better. Oh, I gave her some Latin word for her complaint to satisfy her—just as the priest of olden times would have told her he was chasing out the devil Voluptas, or What-have-you. After that she just *couldn't* stay in bed. It was physically impossible."

"Yes," Mr Verity agreed. "I have to admit that your authority is the firmest: not even the infliction of indignity can shake it."

He looked out at the garden where the butt of Rambler's cigar glowed in the darkness.

"Maxwell's was such an authority too," said the doctor. "You might say it thrived on indignity."

"Yes. I spoke last night of my Sicilian gardener—of a man who took pleasure in destroying what was young and excited and free. I do not speak of insensitivity—that is a crime which by common participation has become a mere fault. On the contrary the man was *too* sensitive: the thing he smashed shamed him by its beauty. I fancy Maxwell as just such a man—a being who felt shamed by the health and charity of other people. Remember that Paxton did his early crime to save a friend, and Miss Burton to help her father."

"I think I agree with you. Such a man contaminates. Both the man and the girl could so easily have recovered if *he* hadn't been there to prevent it."

"And now both lie under suspicion of murder."

"He's an awful warning to us," Pelham said, draining his glass. "We have the power—but sometimes I wonder how long even we will be allowed to keep it."

"Tudor declared to me this morning that power must always be wielded by the few over the many."

"Maybe that is true, but in the last resort the many can revoke it."

"Or it can be revoked in the name of the majority by a higher power."

"I beg your pardon?"

"Let me tell you the legend of my Sea Goddess."

He got up slowly and laid his hand on a gaunt stone head behind him.

"Look at this. This is the Minerva of the Aegean. Years and years ago this figure was washed up by the sea upon the shores of a small village in Greece. Look at her closely: her authority was once unquestioned." He reached for a candle and held it up to the pedestal: the rough face of an old woman stared at them with its hollow eyes. On her brow the hair was coiled like sleeping black snakes; her nose was still straight and beautifully formed, but the mouth—a smooth, round hole—was almost entirely worn away.

"All the villagers worshipped her; she was their guide in all misfortune. At every crisis in a man's affairs he went to this figure, fitted his mouth to her mouth, and sucked up the wisdom from her brain. Of course, as time went on, the mouth grew less and less, and finally became almost as you see it now—worn away by all those many passionate kisses of curiosity. In the end it was decreed that, to save her mouth from further damage by the lips of the people, only the priests might consult her.

"The people were very reluctant to obey, and the elders of the village found it difficult to convince them that this was the wisest course. In the end, however, they agreed. But, so the legend goes, the Sea Goddess grew angry at this order—and from then on she made all her wisdom inaccessible to the wise because they had denied her the embraces of the foolish."

Friday morning saw the hot weather persisting. The grass dew sparkled in the early sun and there was a bloom on the sky.

Mr Rambler and Mr Verity came pounding down the path from 'Persepolis' with the heavy eagerness of mastiffs scenting a poacher. At the outskirts of the town a man approached them, and stood hesitantly in their way. It was Edward Winnidge.

"Can I speak to you for a moment?" he asked.

"Of course!" Verity noticed a haunted, sleepless look in his eyes. "What is it?"

"It's about yesterday. I've been waiting half an hour to tell you this."

"What about yesterday?"

"Well, I know I behaved badly yesterday, and—well, a chap gets flustered with the police round, and one thing and another... My nerves are all on edge, you see, and well..."

"Is this an apology or something more interesting?"

"You see, Alice rang me up last night and told me how kind you'd been, sir—and how you were only trying to help."

He lowered his eyes and stared fixedly at the ground. Mr Verity wondered whether his discomforture rose from the difficulty of expressing gratitude, or that of concealing guilt.

"That's gracious of her," he said aloud.

"Thank you, sir."

"Young man," said Rambler severely, "it is my duty to tell you that Miss Burton is in very serious trouble."

"But surely you believe her?"

"I do not. And I'm not sure I believe you."

The man's face paled with returning anger.

"What I told Mr Verity was the truth. The whole truth!... He said he believed me."

"I am inclined to think most of it was the truth," agreed Rambler.

"He said he had a witness to bear me out!"

"The vicar? Yes, he does bear out part of your story. That's the part I believe."

"But—you don't think I killed him?"

"The thought had occurred to us," admitted Verity. "How is your friend Tudor this morning?"

"Tudor?... I don't understand." Winnidge's voice faltered.

"Well, he can bear you out, too, can't he?"

"Yes! Of course he can!... He can bear me out!"

"That vestibule must have been pretty dark, at six-thirty." Rambler put in, stroking his jaw. "In circumstances like that it is not always easy to tell where a man is wounded: before or behind—on the jaw or in the back."

"But I tell you he *saw*! Don't you understand, Maxwell moved!"

"You are the only one to say so," said Rambler.

"But Tudor can—"

"We have had enough of this," Verity retorted impatiently. "You know as well as anybody that Tudor can tell us nothing."

"What?"

"You must have heard! It's been all over the town. It must even have reached 'The Bellows'."

"No? Is he dead?"

"It's more than likely."

Winnidge went as pale as on the preceding afternoon, when Verity had suggested the possibility of his playing the role of accomplice to Alice.

"I swear I've heard nothing..."

"It is," said Verity, "an affair of major importance at the moment—at any rate as far as you are concerned."

"And even should he round the corner this moment," added Rambler, "you are not out of danger. Very far from it. You see, we are also particularly interested in what you did with Mr Maxwell *after* you took him upstairs. To us the scene heard by Mr Maxwell's neighbour a little after six-thirty in the morning is as important as what passed on the stairs between you and Mr Tudor."

"I—I—."

"Good morning to you, Mr Winnidge," said Verity firmly.

The two men resumed their march to the hotel, leaving the man standing dumbfounded in the sunlight. The news of a neighbour to Maxwell (the attentive Mr Swabber) was evidently quite a shock to Ted Winnidge.

"All the same, I'm glad he apologised for his *brusquerie*," said Verity after a pause. "I like the man."

"So do I," confessed Rambler. "It's a shame—a very great shame."

"I don't understand. What's a shame?"

"Well, things look pretty black for the both of them, you must admit."

"On the contrary. Forgive me for playing mysterious, but as I said last night, I see things rather more in their favour now."

"Even with the disappearance of Tudor?"

"I once told Jackson we'd find that Tudor had very little to do with the case. I still believe that."

"I should say he's just the sort of man to get into trouble."

"No, he's far too used to not being taken seriously to get into very much trouble. He lives in a world of his own that springs a hundred little private sensations on him every day.

Why should he bother with a comparatively petty outrage like the shooting of a blackmailer?"

Rambler said nothing.

"Besides, I was watching Winnidge a minute ago. He was really furious that we didn't believe him."

"Of course he was."

"Yes, but unless he were insane, a guilty man would rather expect our disbelief."

"A minute ago," said Rambler stolidly, "you were implying that Mr Tudor's insanity always led him to expect disbelief."

"Good God!" Verity exploded. "This is no time for conundrums, Porpoise."

"I am merely trying to understand what you are saying."

"Listen. Winnidge was angry—very angry. But it was a bewildered anger. He was wild with us for not believing him. He couldn't understand why we didn't accept his story in all its details."

"And how," asked Rambler seriously, "would you undertake to mark the difference between a man thwarted in telling the truth and one thwarted in telling a lie?"

"He bears the look of an honest man," said Verity. "It is a quality which simply cannot be simulated in my presence."

"I suppose," said Rambler, permitting himself a sarcasm with formal gravity, "that you once found the same look on the face of a stone bust in Greece."

"No," Verity replied, "it was actually in Italy. And the material was Carrara marble."

They entered 'The Charter' together. Jackson was at his table, with Sergeant Matthews.

"Good morning," said Verity. "I want to see Cunningham right away. It's most important."

Matthews was sent for Cunningham.

"What's this for?" asked Rambler.

"Wait. I am about to produce one of the last and largest rabbits from a very bad hat."

Rambler grunted. "Any news of Tudor?"

"None," said Jackson. "I've sent out a description, of course. All we can do is wait, sir."

"Mm."

"Do you think he's done a bolt, sir? If he has, he took a long time to do it."

"Mm."

"Perhaps he only realised the significance of what he saw much later."

"More likely he's just afraid of the police, like the vicar," said Verity. "And all because he didn't come forward with the story of how he met Winnidge in the small hours."

"Withholding evidence seems quite a pastime in this part of the world," said Rambler fiercely.

The door opened and Matthews brought Cunningham into the room.

"Good morning," said Verity affably. "Take a seat."

Mr Cunningham nodded quickly to the three detectives and took his usual place on the wicker settee. Rambler accepted of Verity his first cigar of the day and retired to Jackson's side of the table; Matthews watched impassively from further off. Verity was left holding the floor.

"I've asked you to come back here," he said, after a pause,

"because there are one or two questions I want to put to you."

"Well?"

"Mr Cunningham: who do you think killed Mr Maxwell?"

Cunningham looked up, startled. Verity saw that his hair and moustache were even more unkempt than at the first interview; his eyes too had again lost their power to focus properly.

"What was that you said?"

"I asked you who killed Maxwell."

"What's this?... Still part of the act with your friend?" He turned his wandering eyes on Rambler. "How the hell should I know?"

"Now stop that whining," said Verity crisply. "It won't help you. Now let's have a few guesses, shall we?"

"Guesses?"

"At the murderer. What do you say to Paxton?"

"I say I mind my own business."

"An excellent, if rather a novel, policy."

"What do you mean?"

"Two days ago in this room you accused Paxton fairly definitely of murdering Maxwell—probably in collaboration with Miss Framer."

"I was upset then... I didn't know what I was saying."

"You mean you didn't know you were saying it out loud. That's quite a guarantee that you really meant it."

"I was on edge—nervous... I wasn't responsible," said Cunningham, beginning to get excited.

"Then if you don't think Paxton did it in collaboration with Miss Framer, how about Miss Framer by herself?"

"Miss Framer?"

Jackson, whose suspect she had been all the time, sat up and began sharpening a pencil.

"It's unlikely that she did it, isn't it?" asked Verity. "I mean considering that her prints weren't on the gun we found. It's as unlikely as that Paxton did it and then called the police."

"Here, what are you getting at?… I know you, Verity—this is all a clever way of saying I did it, isn't it?"

"Is it? I was just coming to Miss Burton."

"That waitress?… Now there you have something!" His eyes came to rest on Verity's face with a gleam of excitement. "You saw how she tried to blame it on to me with that story of hers about me dressing up in a mask… And I tell you, I heard her quarrelling with Maxwell only the night before."

"It may interest you to know that I found a mask of black silk yesterday evening—in a drawer in Miss Burton's bedroom."

There was a pause. Then for the first time Cunningham smiled.

"There you are, you see!… It's as plain as a pikestaff!"

"Not to me," said Verity.

"Well, she was going to use it to incriminate me! Don't you understand? I shouldn't be surprised if it was she who dropped that key under my chair in the dining-room."

"That's an interesting hypothesis."

"Yes, isn't it? I mean she could have, just as easily as—"

"Mr Cunningham," said Verity coldly, "why did you put that mask in Miss Burton's room?"

"What!... Me?..."

"You."

"Now look!... Don't be bloody ridiculous!"

He struggled angrily to his feet. Verity sat quite still.

"On Wednesday night," he said slowly, "and on my instructions, Sergeant Matthews searched Miss Burton's room *before she was allowed to go back to it.*"

"My God! I'd forgotten that," cried Rambler, jumping up excitedly. "How could I have been so stupid?"

Verity turned apologetically to Matthews.

"I'm sorry, Sergeant, but this is important. I've told Inspector Jackson already—he knows I took full responsibility."

"That's all right," said Jackson quickly. "You did very well."

"He did excellently," said Verity, springing up, too, and towering over Cunningham. "Excellently! I thought the end had justified the means when the search produced a letter to her from Maxwell. But this is something quite apart! You realise what it means, don't you, Cunningham?... It means that the person who put the mask in her drawer was not Alice Burton."

"She could have had it on her all the time!"

"She was searched—as you were."

"She could have hidden it somewhere!"

"As you could! But listen to this, Mr Cunningham,"—Verity peered hard into his victim's sweaty face—"just listen to this. If Alice Burton had made that mask to incriminate you, would she have left it at the top of her first drawer for anyone to find? Would she? Such details hang people, Mr Cunningham!...

No, the only person who could have put it in so obvious a position is someone who *wanted* it to be found! And could anyone want that more than you?"

"Me?… Why me?… Why should I want to do a thing like that?"

"To make us believe what we were only too inclined to believe already: that Miss Burton fabricated the whole story in order to put the blame on to you. Not so very clever an idea, when all is said and done."

"It's a lie!" Cunningham cried hoarsely. "You're trying to trap me! Paxton could have planted that mask!"

"Paxton didn't even know about the mask!" cried Rambler, coming forward and taking a hand in the inquisition.

"Miss Framer—"

"Miss Framer neither—"

"It's a lie! They both saw the newspapers!"

"You're a bad liar," said Verity coldly, walking away to the window. "Ask yourself what motive would I have for searching Miss Burton's room after I knew it had already been searched efficiently by Sergeant Matthews. I did so because I *knew* that mask was there."

There was dead silence. Cunningham stared at him in terror.

"And I knew also that you put it there."

"No…"

"I watched you plant it."

"You're lying!…"

"It was an amusing idea of yours. You presented Miss Burton with a mask in order to discredit her own story about that mask. The very same mask you wore in Maxwell's room."

"The very same mask…" repeated Cunningham stupidly. "The very same…"

"The very same mask which I *saw* you put in Miss Burton's room."

He made as if to protest, then suddenly closed his mouth.

"The very same mask," said Verity, "in which you killed Maxwell."

Everyone was very still. There was a pause. Then Cunningham nodded quietly.

"You knew you had to kill him if your supply of dope was to continue. You wanted to kill him, too, for the misery he had caused you and for the degradation to which his persecution had brought you. Didn't you?"

"And I would do it over again," said Cunningham slowly, raising his head and looking at Verity with firm grey eyes. "I would do it now—here, in front of you. I am no criminal. You have had to wear me down to get me to admit it, but now that I can speak of it I am happy! I was proud of myself when I had done it. All Wednesday night I lay awake thinking that now not only me, but hundreds of others—hundreds—were free of him. Hundreds just like me, who had gone wrong once and, because of him, had never been allowed to get back… They would never suffer again—never again receive his letters… any more…"

He was in tears. For a long moment no one spoke. Then Verity said:

"Tell me what happened."

He had some difficulty collecting himself, but he finally accepted a cigarette, and Sergeant Matthews got ready to take notes.

"I went to see him," he said in a hushed, low voice. "It was about seven-thirty-five. I listened at the door, but there was no noise."

"You had on your mask?"

"Yes, in case there was anybody in the passage. I had the gun with me. I opened the door and went in. I was going to make one last effort to plead with him about leaving me alone—"

"You mean leaving you and your supplier alone. We shall want his name, of course."

Cunningham nodded.

"You don't know everything. I'd had to steal in order to pay Maxwell and get the stuff as well. I stole quite a bit. And of course he knew about it. He knew everything."

"Go on. Where was he when you went into the room?"

"Sitting in a chair. Miss Burton was—in his arms."

"Ordering breakfast," murmured Verity.

"He got up when I came in. He was frightened, I can tell you… I was glad to see that—but I hadn't bargained on the girl. I told her to go into the corner of the room. After all, what else could I do? I couldn't send her out of the room—not then… And in any case, she didn't know me. I didn't think of the wardrobe then."

"It was still an absurdly ineffective thing to do, if you don't mind my saying so."

"Of course it was… I didn't even know what I was doing…"

"And then?"

"Then I started talking to him. I told him I'd come to plead with him to let me go. I couldn't stand it without the stuff—at least, not right away, not just like that! I told him if my friend stopped supplying me, I couldn't go on living. He said there'd never be any need to tell the police about my friend if I went on paying him. I told him I couldn't. I just couldn't: it was physically impossible to pay him!"

"'I've paid my last shilling to you, Maxwell...'"

"What was that?"

"Nothing. Just a quotation. Go on please."

"Then he laughed, and told me to steal it—as I'd done before; that if I didn't pay him what he wanted, he'd tell the police about that too. Then I went wild. Suddenly the realisation came to me of exactly what he'd done to me... how this one man had deliberately ruined my life." He paused, then went on in a rush: "You don't know what that stuff can do to you... You can't know—but he did. He knew. He knew that I'd do anything to get it—I think he enjoyed that part best of all!... I admit I took dope before I met him, but I was none the worse for that. Not really... But afterwards it was different. There was no escape from him. He made me a liar, a thief and a swindler. He made my life a nightmare—and there was never anywhere I could turn. You see, I had no friends: like him, I had no friends."

"What did you do in that room?" asked Rambler firmly.

"We fought. I killed him."

"How?"

"I shot him as we struggled. In the back. I couldn't believe I'd really done it. I held him up in my arms: he was heavy and didn't move. I had some idea I should take him off the floor—perhaps put him in a chair. But he seemed to flop down all the time—he flopped all round the room. It was almost like the struggle again. His blood started staining the walls when I propped him up against them... Have you ever tried to hold a dead body upright? It's difficult."

"You did all this in front of the girl?"

"I don't know how much she saw. I was so wild I didn't care at the time. Afterwards, when I cooled down a bit, I found she'd fainted. I realised that she'd probably seen everything."

"And you had to make a get-away?"

"That's why I put her in the cupboard. I found some cord and tied up her hands and feet, but not too tightly. Then I shut the door on her."

"What did you do with the key?"

"I put it in beside her. I didn't want any more trouble—and there was just a chance neither she nor Maxwell would be missed, for some time."

"And then you left?"

"No, not just then. I saw a man on the balcony outside. It was Paxton, and he was preparing to climb into the room. What could I do?... I was so frightened... I hid."

"Where?"

"Behind the bed. I waited while he came in. I heard him gasp when he saw the body. Then he came over and messed around for a bit on the floor. Finally he bolted out of the room and down the stairs, calling like the devil for the police."

"Did he touch the gun on the floor?"

"I don't know. I couldn't see."

"What happened then? You left by the window?"

"Yes, I knew the door wasn't safe."

"Did you lock the ordinary door?"

"I don't think so."

"But you left the gun," said Rambler.

"Yes, I'd forgotten all about it by that time. I climbed out of the window as fast as I could. There was blood all over my fingers and on my coat. I remember that I put streaks of it on the window as I went: it was horrible."

"It was brilliant," said Verity. "We thought it was Maxwell's own traces."

"And then down the pipe into the arms of the constable?" asked Rambler, for neatness' sake.

"Yes. He saw the mask in my top-pocket, but he thought it was my pocket-handkerchief."

Verity laughed. "And that's the story?"

"Yes. And now do what you please. I'm not afraid of anything."

Jackson looked at Rambler. Rambler looked at Verity; Verity looked at Matthews and said, in his gentlest tone:

"Take Mr Cunningham into the dining-room and give him some coffee, will you?"

Cunningham got to his feet.

"You're a clever man, Mr Verity," he said.

"Yes," said Mr Verity. "I remember reflecting yesterday that you were a man whom one could easily bluff if need be. And need was."

"I don't understand."

"I am afraid I practised a deception on you a little earlier on this morning, Mr Cunningham. I trust you will forgive me

when you view it in the light of its success. You see I told you
I saw you enter Miss Burton's room with the mask."

"What?"

"Well, I didn't."

CHAPTER XI

"AND YET EVEN THIS ISN'T GOOD ENOUGH," SAID THE old man, scattering pebbles into the garden pool. "Not even a signed confession can explain away that locked window."

"And that locked door," said Jackson. "He still thinks he didn't touch it."

"And all the London Press is waiting," sighed Verity. "Poor Jackson! You have a murderer self-confessed—and the girl who alone could have helped him to do it, he says he trussed up with cord. I'm afraid everything still centres on the woman in the wardrobe."

Rambler spoke, sadly fingering his jowl.

"If only he hadn't mentioned her quarrelling with Maxwell on the Tuesday night, and if only she hadn't denounced him as the man in the mask!... Then we could safely say he was shielding her: and from our standpoint, everything in the garden would be lovely!"

"Everything in the garden *is* lovely!" said Verity, striding away through the long grass to the apple-tree. "There's nothing for me quite so summery as the sight of ripening apples, swelling and reddening at the same time—like a regiment of colonels very slowly getting worked up about the national situation."

"It's all such a mess," said Rambler suddenly.

Jackson looked startled. It was the first discouraged word he had heard him use. In the pool the absurd silver fish sank to the bottom, and the gleam departed from their scales.

"An hour ago," said Verity, "you were absolutely sure that Alice Burton and Ted Winnidge had done it between them:— only because you had forgotten that I had asked Sergeant Matthews to search her room earlier on. (I'm sorry, by the way, I didn't jog your memory earlier, but I couldn't resist a *coup de théâtre*.) Now—with the addition of that one more fact—you instantly believe that Cunningham did it."

"Two more facts," said Rambler shortly. "He admits he did."

"Well, the answer seems to me to be obvious. The more facts you gather, the more of the truth you learn. There's a metaphysic there somewhere."

"You mean we should all start hunting for more evidence?"

"Yes, I mean just that, Porpoise. We want to do some more solid detecting."

"In what direction, may I ask?"

"Ah, if we knew that there'd be no difficulty! But you're right: as usual, it's thought before action. Now consider, this is really very interesting." He stretched himself at full length on the grass. "The facts we have already are not enough, but they're the only things that can tell us where to look for more. It's rather like playing a treasure-hunt in which one of the clues has a dual significance. Its first function is to lead you to the next clue in the normal way; but its second function only becomes clear when you've reached the penultimate stage: it is to lead you straight to the treasure. We have now reached that stage, and I'm afraid we'll have to go back over the ground, looking for the clue."

There was a pause.

"I'm afraid I don't understand," said Jackson blankly.

"Mr Verity means," explained Rambler, "that what we need is one clue that *only now* makes full sense."

"I see, sir," said Jackson.

"Or," said Verity suddenly stiffening, "we want one clue that only now has ceased to make any sense at all."

He got up excitedly.

"I'm sorry to put it so paradoxically," he said to Jackson, who was looking mutinous, "but the fact is I couldn't have expressed it more neatly."

"No, sir."

"Expressed what?" asked Rambler.

"Something I've just remembered."

"And that is?"

"I must have time to think. And I must be alone to do it."

He moved quickly to the garden gate.

"Where are you going?"

"Into the sea. A bathe will probably help a great deal."

"But you haven't a costume!"

"I know. I left it behind deliberately. Yesterday the sea was too warm. Today it will be warmer still—much too hot for a bathing-costume. No one," said Mr Verity triumphantly, "can say I don't learn from experience."

The day wore on. Lunch was served and eaten. For Jackson the afternoon was occupied in getting down Cunningham's statement and preparing a report. For Rambler it was spent in profound thought in the living-room at 'Persepolis', under the disdainful scrutiny of the statues.

As for the other erstwhile suspects, Miss Framer sat talking earnestly with Mr Paxton under the shade of the apple-tree; and Alice Burton and Ted Winnidge walked the beach, hand-in-hand, and watched Mr Verity from afar with a sense of overwhelming awe. The formidable old man lay on his back, motionless upon the broad sea.

When at length he rose from it—like some paunchy triton in whose beard the sea-drops sparkled—and made, naked and shaking, for the sand, his two observers retreated scandalised into the garden of 'The Charter'. Here the old man soon joined them, re-dressed in flannels, but failed in his abstraction to see either them, or the older couple beneath the tree. He passed straight across the lawn, strode into the hotel, and disappeared up the stairs. He was there for over an hour. On descending he ordered Jackson to assemble everybody in the lounge for eight that evening.

Returning across the grass, he was accosted by Mr Paxton.

"Excuse me," he said, "but could you possibly tell me when I will be allowed to leave this hotel?" His eyes stared anxiously through the lenses of his thick-framed spectacles. "I have much to do now."

"I daresay you have," said Verity coolly. "However, we must first determine whether you go to jail charged with murder, or merely with attempted murder."

"But—"

"Subject yourself to the higher powers, my good sir."

He passed on, but was intercepted by Alice.

"Mr Verity—"

"Later."

"There's something we must know."

"Tonight at eight."

He brushed by them to the beach and sat by himself on a sand-dune, at the distance of two hundred yards from the gate, looking out to sea. The smoke of his cigars curled endlessly into the empyrean.

In the course of the afternoon the journalists of the day before returned, together with a protesting embassy from *The Yardstick*. But their attempts to see Verity were frustrated less by the police, who had strict instructions to admit no one to his presence, than by his own apparent cataleptic trance when they finally burst through the cordon of his guards and rushed along the beach to interview him. He seemed neither to hear nor to see them, and he moved at all only to knock the ash from his cigar. Miss Framer herself tried to bring him some tea and sandwiches, but was likewise dismissed.

Towards evening a great hush fell on 'The Charter': in the silence and failing light, the lounge filled obediently with those of its inmates who were concerned. Alice and Ted sat on the settee, Paxton and the Manageress in adjoining armchairs. Cunningham, farther off, felt the pressure of social ostracism in the form of a high-backed chair; and behind him stood Constable Locksley and the constable who had first caught him at the bottom of the drain-pipe. Jackson himself sat at the large table which all along had served for his desk: it had been dragged a little from the centre of the room to leave a space between the Law and those now immediately subject to it.

At the last moment Rambler came in and went straight to the far corner of the room, where he sat down in the deepest armchair and remained silent. Colonel Rainchart looked in, but was promptly asked to leave; in the end he did, but still declaring fractiously that it was the concern of every right-thinking man and woman.

Eight o'clock struck. All buzz of conversation died away as Mr Verity was seen moving slowly across the garden towards them. He entered the room and stood for a moment in silence before the table, facing the assembled company. He looked very tired, and the lids hung heavily over his dulled eyes. At length he said:

"As you know, Mr Cunningham has confessed to the murder of the late Mr Maxwell. Some of you may think this is sufficient reason for the police to pursue the case no further and, ordinarily, it probably would be. But in the present case this is not the whole story: you are about to hear the end of it now. I hope it will clear up in your minds some of the mysteries that this affair has created: it will certainly reveal another killer."

His hearers shifted nervously in their seats and waited.

"Let me start the story from the beginning," he said. "It all began when Miss Burton sought refuge from Mr Maxwell's threats and embraces in the town of Amnestie. By doing so she started this whole complicated train of events. Believe me, the Woman in the Wardrobe has much to answer for. She came down here and took a job as a waitress at 'The Charter'.

She explained her move in a letter to Maxwell: she told him about her fiancé, and thereby involved him as well."

Winnidge made an attempt to protest, but Verity stopped him with a gesture.

"I want no interruptions, please. Mr Maxwell followed her down here and stayed at the same hotel. On his reappearance Miss Burton's noble resolve to have things out, and to tell him to do his worst, faltered. She tried to compromise; in fact she let things go on from day to day: and all the time she permitted herself to be pawed as she served him his kidneys, her young lover remaining in complete ignorance."

"Is this strictly necessary?" Winnidge shouted.

"When I asked her why this was she told me she 'wanted time to think'. What she wanted was time to think of a way out—but it took her four days to realise that there never was a way out with Maxwell. It took her one last quarrel with him to realise that she had no chance whatever of escaping from the net, except by cutting it. Then, by her own confession, she rushed off to Mr Winnidge and urged him to kill Maxwell."

"Now look here—"

"She says she didn't know what she was saying but, as I have observed before in another context, that rarely signifies that she did not mean it."

A murmur of alarm and protest passed round the room.

"This is all just an attack on us!" Winnidge called above it.

"There is much to attack," said Verity equably. "However, let us leave this for the moment and see what else your girl did."

The group in the room murmured again. Winnidge swore and sprang forward; Verity shrugged and stayed fast. The young man was finally constrained to sit down by a policeman, and his arm was taken firmly by his fiancée, who looked horridly pale and muttered something imploringly in his ear.

"Her coming down here," Mr Verity resumed, "brought Maxwell after her: and his coming brought Mr Paxton on the Monday, and Mr Cunningham on the Tuesday. We found the draft letters which Maxwell wrote to these two close friends of his from here, and omitted to throw away. And finally there was Miss Framer. Perhaps I had better explain this a little."

Paxton stiffened in his chair and looked straight ahead. Miss Framer's eyes were shut tight.

"Several years ago now, Miss Framer allowed herself to be extricated from an embarrassing position by means of an illegal expedient, thought out for her by a legal mind. This expedient cost Mr Paxton his career because, unfortunately, his precautions were inadequate to prevent Mr Maxwell's securing proof of the details. Blackmail inevitably ensued. After about ten years, unlike Mr Paxton, Miss Framer managed to free herself from it by disappearing: she went, of course, into this part of the world—where she successfully ran 'The Charter' for almost a year, and even managed to improve what is obscurely called its 'tone'. It was her misfortune that Alice Burton also chose this particular hotel in which to hide. Or shall we say that it was her misfortune that Mr Winnidge had his home here? Anyway, Maxwell arrived and soon recognised the poor woman. As I see it, he reserved to himself the pleasure of dealing with this old victim after he had settled matters with the new. A note among his papers refers only very briefly to 'Miss F'. Fortunately for her, he was too busy with Miss Burton to attack her before he died."

"No," said Paxton quietly. "He did attack her. Through me. I was to start what he called 'negotiations'."

"Of course! Hence the whispering so frequently described by Mr Cunningham. I was regarding these merely as attempts to calm her."

"She was in a terrible state," said Paxton.

He put out a hand and touched her arm.

"Of course," said Verity. "So by her coming down here, Miss Burton involved all these people within the area of a small hotel. Thus far the chronology of events is pretty clear." He looked about him, but no one offered any contradiction.

"From Friday to Tuesday Miss Burton vacillated and Miss Framer trembled for the renewal of Maxwell's attack. On Monday Paxton arrived, doubtless saw Maxwell, and attempted to defy him: he was told that he must continue, and that his ex-client must resume payment."

Paxton sighed audibly.

"On Tuesday the tension must have been noticeably increasing. Mr Paxton and Miss Framer are in desperation; Miss Burton is making a final appeal to Maxwell; Mr Cunningham arrives with a gun. Miss Framer sees it when it is inadvertently dropped in the vestibule, and tells Mr Paxton. What hope they must have felt in their hearts!... An hour afterwards Miss Burton, blazing with fury and hate, is on her way to see her lover. The preliminaries are over. And now what happens?"

There was a pause while Mr Verity lit a cigar. A ray of the dying sun stained his face bronze.

"This is where we went astray," he said at last. "I admit it. But it was not our fault. All the facts we discovered pointed to one solution: that Alice Burton and Edward Winnidge murdered Maxwell between them. At one time we believed that Winnidge shot him in Amnestie Square by the side of his taxi, using a gun with a silencer. We believed that, realising the wound was not fatal, he carried his victim upstairs and shot him again. We further believed that he then searched the room for a letter he had earlier written to Maxwell which would have revealed to the investigating police a connection between the two men: and that, failing to find it, he went to Alice's room and told her he had killed Maxwell—as she had ordered him to do—and then rehearsed her in a plan to put all the blame on to Mr Cunningham. The only way we could explain the mystery of the locked door and the locked window was by assuming a plan that had been bungled in its execution. You may think this seems absurd, but everything supported it:—the vicar's story, the stain at the foot of the stairs, the prints on the gun, the fantastic story of the man in the mask, and the subsequent denunciation of Mr Cunningham as that man. In fact, if I hadn't done something rather unorthodox, young man and young maid would both have had a very unpleasant time of it."

Murmurs of undirected indignation broke out, which the old man ignored.

"As it was, I asked one of Inspector Jackson's men to search Miss Burton's room before allowing her to get back to it. That was how I knew the mask I discovered there next day had been planted on her. It was this knowledge that made nonsense of our suspicions, and enabled me to bluff Mr Cunningham. Now, you see, I had to work from the other end—*from an assumption of Mr Cunningham's guilt.* The thing to do, as Inspector Rambler had suggested, was to find a clue which only now made sense. I did it the other way round and found one which by now made nonsense. I do not count the mystery of the locked door and window—that had made nonsense all along. No, I mean Miss Burton's finger-prints on Mr Cunningham's gun. If his story were true—and I was assuming it was—how did those prints get there?"

Detective Inspector Rambler nodded slowly from the gloom. Otherwise all was still in the lounge; the ring of suspects sat motionless, their eyes scrutinising the carpet. Beyond the window the trees were twittering in thickening twilight.

"If she did not touch the gun in that room," said Verity "then she must have touched it somewhere else. And where else had it been, save in Mr Cunningham's bedroom? So I went to Mr Cunningham's bedroom and, after some time, and by a lucky chance, I moved a cupboard that stands against the wall. And there I found what I was looking for. Miss Burton, will you tell me, please, what happened in Mr Cunningham's bedroom on the Tuesday night?"

She nodded, and disengaged herself quickly from Winnidge's grasp.

"All right."

The others looked at her with hostile interest. Mr Verity regretted it was too dark to read expressions.

"Go on," he said.

"We're a bit short of staff at the moment, and Miss Framer asked me whether I'd mind turning down some of the beds. I said I didn't mind. I went into Mr Cunningham's bedroom about half-past ten. He was taking a bath, I think—at any rate he wasn't there. Just as I'd finished removing the coverlet I noticed something sticking out from under the pillow. I took it out."

"And because the idea of killing was uppermost in your mind, you held it in your hands?"

"Yes."

"And finally you even pulled the trigger?"

Alice hung her head.

"The bullet passed through the opposite wall into the room next door. This is disused at the moment and stored with empty boxes, and that kind of thing. Then you hastily replaced the gun and shifted the cupboard over a few inches to hide the hole in the wall."

Miss Burton nodded again.

"And then?"

"Then I opened the window. The room was full of fumes."

"I am scarcely surprised."

"I don't know what made me do it. I…" Winnidge came mutely to the rescue. But Verity continued relentlessly.

"I suppose you thought you were lucky that the hole was so near the cupboard that a shift of a few inches would cover it. I suppose, too, you thought yourself lucky that Mr

Cunningham never examined his revolver? Foolish girl! Such pieces of luck almost hanged you."

Jackson interrupted: "You said you were expecting to find this hole, sir. How was this?"

"The high incidence-rate of significant cupboards in her life, I suppose," said Verity, smiling.

"Yes, sir."

"I'll tell you the proper reason in a moment. Let me retrace the thing in my own way. I hope you are not observing a lack of coherence in my narrative?"

"No, sir."

"Good. Well then, let me describe to you what happened in that bedroom between seven-thirty and eight o'clock. At half-past seven Mr Maxwell, recovering from the severe blow Winnidge had given him earlier on, rings the bell for his favourite waitress. She is calmer by the morning, and even submits to the usual advances. Mr Cunningham finds them together: he is dressed in his mask and carries his gun. Miss Burton is relegated to the corner; the argument develops between the two men; and finally Mr Cunningham fires and wounds Maxwell in the back. Mr Cunningham has told us of the difficulty he had to keep him upright after the shooting—it was almost like a struggle, he said. Actually it *was* a struggle: a wounded man was shamming dead in the arms of his terrified assailant. Once Maxwell realised he wasn't dead, pretence became his only hope of escape.

"Miss Burton faints. Swiftly Cunningham moves over to her, trusses her up, and bundles her into the wardrobe. Just as he finishes he sees Paxton coming, and hides. Paxton comes in. He makes the mistake of taking Maxwell to be dead—and of handling Cunningham's gun. So he runs off for the police, and Cunningham departs by the window."

"I admit it!" said Paxton. "I didn't even stop to examine him. I just assumed it. There was all that blood about, you see—and the mess in the room. I was terrified! I didn't know what to think…"

"Yes, I remember you were rather unnerved. All the same, you realise that I had to establish by deduction what your ordinary powers of observation could have told me in the normal way, if only you had taken the time to apply them! At the least you might have remembered how many wounds the man had in his back."

"There was too much blood about," said Paxton doggedly. "He might have had a dozen bullets in his back for all I knew."

"Well, in point of fact, he only had one. Maxwell was, as I say, still alive. He could not have been dead when you saw him—"

"Could not?" said Jackson.

"No, because he was the only man who could have locked the door and bolted the window from the inside."

"What was that?"

The Inspector looked puzzled, and almost determined not to comprehend.

Verity repeated his remark.

"I had entertained the idea before, of course, but there were too many things against it. A moment ago, Inspector, you asked me how I knew what to look for in Mr Cunningham's bedroom. Well, to assume that Maxwell was still alive after both Paxton and Cunningham had departed was the only logical solution. There was nothing impossible in this: Dr Pelham had told us quite clearly that one of the two bullets found in Maxwell had been fatal. The other was comparatively harmless. Obviously, then, Mr Cunningham had fired only one bullet—the comparatively harmless. He himself was too worked up to know how many bullets he had fired at the time of the shooting!"

Cunningham was staring at him dumbfounded: he looked as if he were about to go down on his knees.

"Yet two bullets had most certainly been fired from that gun. And thinking about them, I suddenly made sense out of nonsense. I realised how Miss Burton had managed to put her prints on the handle. It was at that point that I left the sea and went off to explore Mr Cunningham's room. The rest must be obvious to you."

If it was, no one said anything.

"When Cunningham had climbed out of the window and disappeared down the drain-pipe, Maxwell staggered to his feet. The bullet must have been causing him much pain, and the wound bled a great deal. He must surely have believed that Paxton, entering secretively through the window, had also intended to kill him, and had only left because he believed him to be dead already. Yet supposing one or the other returned? Supposing Cunningham were not convinced he had really killed him? Or Paxton came to have another look? At all costs they must be kept out!... Desperately the man staggers to the window and bolts it. Then he rushes back and locks the door, throwing the key across the floor. Then, all his strength exhausted, he flops down on his knees before the door and listens. The noises outside increase. First he hears Paxton and myself on the other side of the door—Paxton banging on it for all he's worth. Then Cunningham calling from the hall!... But he is safe! The door is locked and the window bolted!

"The police arrive, but the unfamiliar voice of Inspector Jackson only adds to his fear—the last thing he'll do will be to open that door. No, instead he squats against it, speechless with terror. Miss Framer has lost her pass-key: yet the door must be opened. And so in all haste the lock is shot off from the outside with Paxton's unused revolver—and a .45 bullet, fired at point-blank range, smashes through an old hotel lock and pursues its irresistible way into Maxwell's back. It enters his heart, and he is instantly killed."

He paused a moment, and then said softly:

"With only one of Mr Cunningham's bullets found in Maxwell's body, I had to account for the other one. I trust I have done it satisfactorily."

"But one bullet came from Mr Cunningham's gun and one from Mr Paxton's," objected Jackson after a pause.

"True," answered Verity. "Both came from Jessop's, in the Strand."

There was a dreadful silence. Then Jackson coughed, and scratched his head, and at length said slowly:

"And if I may ask, sir, who shot the lock off that door?"

"I did," said Mr Verity.

CHAPTER XII

THE SUN HAD LONG SET. TWILIGHT WAS DYING ON THE sea, and on the wash of the sky. Mr Rambler walked with Mr Verity along the dark blue beach.

"You know," said Rambler gently, "I went up to your house this afternoon. I thought it all out for myself among your statues."

"You knew, then?"

"I knew. But you had to tell them."

"Yes. But—wasn't the pattern perfect?"

Rambler nodded. A man was approaching them from the direction of the hotel. It was Dr Pelham.

"Hullo there!" he cried. "Hullo! I have news for you!"

"Yes?" said Verity. "What now?"

"It's about Richard Tudor."

"You've found him?"

"Certainly I have."

"Good. Now the pattern really is complete. He's not dead, by any chance?"

"No, very much alive: he's in Bognor Regis. He went there on Thursday afternoon—directly after his talk with you in the morning. In fact you seem to have driven him to it."

"To be driven to Bognor Regis isn't so hard a fate as all that. What more am I responsible for?"

"Well, I'm not quite sure. He says that after he talked to you he realised that there was no support to be gained for his cause from the intelligentsia. Up to that point he had apparently thought there was."

"Quite rightly. Messrs. Simnel and Warbeck would have been nowhere without the intellectuals."

"Anyway, you struck him as a flippant and cynical person—'thoroughly representative of your kind'."

"Insulting man!" said Verity.

"'We have no use for such people', he told me, 'no use at all.'"

"Nor will the police after tonight. I do feel out of things. What happened then?"

"Well, you were the last straw, it seems, that broke the camel's back. He decided to renounce the intelligentsia once and for all and put his trust in the common people. So he did. He went to Bognor, and set up his standard in the main street."

"Good Lord!"

"Yes. He even had the Tudor Rose emblazoned on the banner."

"And what did the people of Bognor do?"

"I'm afraid they behaved very badly. When they discovered that he wasn't preaching the Second Coming, they called the police at once. He was in prison by seven this evening. He wouldn't give any name, but kept citing me as someone who would vouch for his sanity. So they sent for me."

"And did you vouch for his sanity?"

"Most certainly I did. I told the police of Bognor that he had documents to prove what he said. So they simply charged him with making a disturbance and let it go at that."

"You behaved with Christian charity, Doctor. It's hard to be fined a couple of pounds for trying to reclaim one's own property."

"By the way," said the doctor, "I hear the Maxwell case is closed. Congratulations."

"I did it," explained Verity simply.

"That's what I meant. Congratulations. What will they call it, by the way?"

"An accident in the course of duty," suggested Rambler.

"Excellent," Pelham commented, "if a little inaccurate. As I see it—as all of them back at the hotel see it—the accident *was* the course of duty."

"You are very kind. However, I have not done unalleviated good."

"I don't understand. Alice and Winnidge are free. So are Paxton and Miss Framer. And you have even saved Cunningham's life when he himself thought it was well lost."

"I was thinking of Jackson."

"Ah yes, poor man! To be baulked like that on his first big case was a little hard."

"Very hard."

"True," Rambler agreed. "He did do all the spade-work."

"And I am sensible of having given him a succession of unworkable patches to till."

"It is really very regrettable," said the doctor, cocking his head sympathetically on one side. "And there's not likely to be another murder in the locality for at least twenty years."

"Murder?" queried Verity.

"I beg your pardon!—accident."

"Of course."

A shadow passed by in the dusk, upright and vigorous.

"Detectives!" it barked derisively.

A little dog tore after it along the sand.

"What a shame!" said Verity when they were alone again, "that we couldn't have made it suicide."

"Too many people know," said Rambler gloomily. "It would have been impossible. And in any case it would have leaked out."

"I was thinking," interjected Pelham, "couldn't you get Cunningham to tell you the name of his dope-pedlar? Then Jackson could proceed with that case and make an arrest on his own."

"Admirable, Doctor! Thank you very much! Admittedly it's a little enough prize for him compared with what might have been, but it's better than nothing."

"And you wouldn't even have got that if you had called it suicide," added Rambler. "You would have had to let Cunningham keep his secret to make sure he didn't divulge yours."

"In a way it's a pity," said Pelham sadly, "that all the others have suffered so much already—otherwise you could have given Jackson the task of looking into their past lives and arresting them for old thefts and cooked alibis. He would have been promoted in no time. But I suppose that's impossible now?"

"Quite," said Rambler.

"Conformity to the Law," said Verity, "would destroy all the irony in such altruism."

"Perhaps you are right. Then the Inspector will have to content himself with some wretched unknown in the back streets of Soho. It'll teach him fortitude. Now if you'll excuse me, I shall say good-night and thank you once again. Come to dinner with me tomorrow night. You'll meet Mrs Treacher— the ex-patient I was telling you about. I've put her on a diet of two very green apples a meal till the end of the month. And she eats four meals a day."

"Delighted!... An admirable man," said Verity, looking after him approvingly as the little doctor retreated briskly up the beach. The sound of the sea reached them close at hand: the same sea that had swallowed up those doughty Lancastrians so many years before. "A really perceptive man. Come, Porpoise: the evening is almost done. Walk with me a little while I enjoy the last cigar of a tiring day... You know, all along I declared that I was on the side of the murderer. I made no attempt to conceal it from anyone, and yet no one believed me. How pleasant it would be—how really pleasant—just for once to be taken at one's face value."

Mr Rambler nodded gravely. Mr Verity lit his cigar. Two fat men walked arm-in-arm by a hyacinthine sea.

THE END

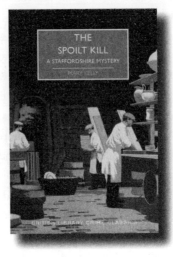

The grey eyes, so apt for tragedy, looked steadily up at me.
"You can't trust me, can you?" she said.

Shentall's, a long-established institution of the Staffordshire Potteries industry, is under attack. With its designs leaked to international competition and its prices undercut, private investigator Hedley Nicholson has been tasked with finding the culprit of the suspected sabotage.

But, industrial espionage may just be the beginning. Delving further into the churning heart of Shentall's Pottery, Nicholson's prying is soon to unearth rumours of bonds cruelly smashed to pieces, grievances irrevocably baked in stone and a very real body, turning and turning in the liquid clay.

First published in 1961, *The Spoilt Kill* received widespread critical acclaim and praise from contemporary crime writers such as Julian Symons. It was awarded the CWA Gold Dagger and remains a finely crafted masterpiece of the crime genre.

ALSO AVAILABLE

In Bloomsbury, London, Inspector Brook of Scotland Yard looks down at a dismal scene. The victim of a ruthless murder lies burnt beyond recognition, his possessions and papers destroyed by fire. But there is one strange, yet promising, lead – a lead which suggests the involvement of a skier.

Meanwhile, piercing sunshine beams down on the sparkling snow of the Austrian Alps, where a merry group of holidaymakers are heading towards Lech am Arlberg. Eight men and eight women take to the slopes, but, as the C.I.D. scrambles to crack the perplexing case in Britain, the ski party are soon to become sixteen suspects.

This exciting, and now extremely rare, mystery novel was first published in 1952, one year after the author's own excursion to the Austrian Alps.

BRITISH LIBRARY CRIME CLASSICS

ALSO AVAILABLE

...titles are also available in eBook, large print and audio editions